Thomas Joseph Potter

Legends, Lyrics and Hymns

Thomas Joseph Potter

Legends, Lyrics and Hymns

ISBN/EAN: 9783744766326

Printed in Europe, USA, Canada, Australia, Japan

Cover: Foto ©Andreas Hilbeck / pixelio.de

More available books at **www.hansebooks.com**

LEGENDS, LYRICS,

AND

HYMNS.

BY

REV. THOMAS J. POTTER,

Author of "The Rector's Daughter," "The Two Victories,"
etc., etc.

DUBLIN:

JAMES DUFFY, 7, WELLINGTON-QUAY,

AND

22, PATERNOSTER-ROW, LONDON.

1862.

DUBLIN:

Printed by J. M. O'Toole and Son,

GREAT BRUNSWICK-STREET.

To

THE HOLY RELIGIOUS,

WHOSE LIVES AND TALENTS ARE DEDICATED TO THE

MERITORIOUS AND ALL-IMPORTANT WORK

OF TRAINING UP THE CHILDREN OF GOD IN THE WAY IN

WHICH THEY OUGHT TO WALK,

THIS LITTLE VOLUME OF VERSES

Is Inscribed

WITH EVERY SENTIMENT OF AFFECTION AND RESPECT.

PREFACE.

———

THIS little book of verses is presented to the public as the third volume of a series, designed principally for the innocent amusement and instruction of Catholic youth, and of which "The Two Victories," and "The Rector's Daughter," form the first numbers.

As the issuing of a volume of poems as one of a series, whose object is so professedly humble, may, perhaps, at first sight, appear somewhat ambitious or misplaced, I deem it necessary to offer a word of explanation as to the motives which have influenced me in taking this step. During the last few years I have occasionally occupied my leisure moments in writing simple poems, sometimes for college purposes, and sometimes as contributions to the various Catholic periodicals of the day. I have frequently been urged to publish these poems in a collected form; and influenced quite as much by the solicitations of, it may be, partial friends, as by my own inclinations, I have at length done so.

I have selected from my published poems such as I deemed suited to the object of this little volume. To these I have added a number of new ones, "England and Rome,"

"The Prayer of St. Patrick," "The Legend of St. Edward and the Irish Cripple," "Eveline," and several others, which are now published for the first time. The hymns which appear at the end of the volume are translations from the Roman Vesperal. These translations were undertaken several years ago for the "Catholic Psalmist," from which work they are now selected. In attempting them, two conditions were put upon me—viz., that the hymns should be rendered as literally as possible, and that the original metre should be preserved as exactly as the difference of the two languages would allow, in order that the airs assigned to the Latin originals in the "Psalmist," might be equally available for the hymns in their English dress, and thus render them useful for novenas and other like functions. In endeavouring to carry out these ideas, I need scarcely say how many minor elegancies of diction, or turns of thought, had to be sacrificed; but, on the other hand, there is not one of the English hymns which cannot be sung to the air to which the corresponding Latin original is set; and the utility of this arrangement is sufficiently proved by the fact, that the translations are frequently thus employed by those who find both devotion and pleasure in the use of English hymns, while the satisfaction with which they are used is certainly not lessened in the mind of a pious and sincere Catholic, by the reflection that they are translated, as closely as it is possible to render one language into another, from the authorized songs of the Church.

Without having the presumption either to expect or believe that this little volume will find much favour with the learned or the critic—if by any chance it may fall into the hands of such—I nevertheless have reason to expect that there arc many to whom it will be welcome, and who will smile kindly upon its advent. As it is intended for this latter class, I think I may venture to say, without any undue pretence of despising their opinion, that I am comparatively indifferent as to its reception by the former. If it succeed in amusing and entertaining those for whom it is intended, it will have attained its end, and its author will have no further anxiety concerning it.

In regard to the poems themselves, of course it scarcely becomes me to speak. If I claim any merit for them, it is merely that of extreme simplicity, both of thought and of treatment. No doubt it would be a great deal better if every one who reads poetry would read Milton or Shakespeare; but there are many readers who find but little entertainment in these works, from the very fact that they are too high—too sublime for them. To such simple people—people, who while they do not, or cannot find entertainment in the works of the great masters in the divine art, still desire and look for poetry of a simple character—I venture humbly to offer this little volume. In every one of the original poems which it contains, I have merely proposed to myself to tell a simple story, or to give expression to a simple idea, in the very simplest manner; but I feel certain that the poems will be none the less acceptable to the great majority of the readers for whom they are intended on this account. For the same reasons I have not employed any of those uncommon metres, or fanciful far-fetched turns of thought, which have occupied so prominent a place in much modern poetry.

It only remains for me to beg from the Catholic public,

and especially from the guardians of youth, for whom, as I have said, these volumes are especially intended, some small share of that kind favour which has been so plentifully bestowed, and to a degree far beyond my expectations, upon "The Two Victories," and "The Rector's Daughter;" and this, not only in these countries, but also upon the Continent, translations of those works having already been issued by the first Catholic publishing houses in France and Belgium.

With these explanatory remarks, I submit my little book, with great diffidence, to the Catholic public. If I shall be judged to have failed, I trust that the object which I had in view will be my apology for the attempt, as it will surely be my own greatest encouragement and support. I again repeat, that I claim as little for my book as it is possible to claim for any work which is worth publishing at all ; but if I, at least, did not hope that my book were worth publishing (and always, of course, considered in relation to the end for which it is intended), it would be great presumption on my part thus to intrude it upon my readers.

T. J. P.

THE DEFINITION

OF

THE IMMACULATE CONCEPTION;

OR,

ENGLAND AND ROME.

B

ENGLAND AND ROME.

HIS Poem was written several years ago, at the request of a friend, to be spoken at the Feast of Languages, which is annually celebrated in the Propaganda College at Rome, on the Festival of the Epiphany. The subject was suggested by the recent definition of the Immaculate Conception of the Blessed Virgin Mary. As will be at once gathered from a perusal of the Poem, it was intended to be recited by an English student, one who might naturally be supposed to speak of the vicissitudes of the past, as well as of the glorious future which is again opening before the English Church.

This Poem is now published for the first time.

THE DEFINITION

OF

𝕿𝖍𝖊 𝕴𝖒𝖒𝖆𝖈𝖚𝖑𝖆𝖙𝖊 𝕮𝖔𝖓𝖈𝖊𝖕𝖙𝖎𝖔𝖓;

OR,

ENGLAND AND ROME.

———◆———

I.

THE morning sun is rising
 O'er the "City of the West,"
With many a bright and golden ray,
 From out the ocean's breast;
And tower, and spire, and palace dome,
 Look fresh, and gay, and bright,
As they shine in all the beauty
 Of the gentle morning light.

II.

'Tis early morn—but Rome's old streets
 Are busy with a throng,
That speeds with keen and eager glance,
 With hasty steps along;

Expectant hope seems smiling bright,
In every beaming eye,
As young and old, and rich and poor,
In gladness hurry by.

III.

On still they rush—that joyous throng
The sons of every clime;
The bishop, with his hoary locks
White with the snows of time:
While many a young and throbbing heart
Is throbbing quicker now,
And nobler shows the noble front
Of many a lofty brow.

IV.

But, lo! they reach that noble pile,
The glory of old Rome;
And countless bands come gath'ring fast,
Beneath its wond'rous dome;
Saint Peter's aisles may scarcely hold
The throng that presses in;
Thrice happy he, who on this day,
Admittance there may win.

V.

In very truth, no common feast
  Is keeping there to-day ;
No common feast, o'er such a mass,
  May hold such mystic sway.
But Mary's sons have gathered there,
  From out of every land,
To place her crown on Mary's brow,
  With glad and willing hand.

*   *   *   *   *   *

VI.

And, soft, *He* comes, that grand old man,
  The ruler of the world,
Whom, from his throne, mad rage and hate,
  Full often would have hurl'd.
With jewelled mitre on his head,
  And crozier in his grasp,
And looks of love, that all the world
  Within their compass clasp.

VII.

He standeth there with Israel's chiefs,
  In prayer, around his feet ;
Where'er he turns, the church's sons
  His glist'ning vision greet.

Full fifty thousand crowd to-day
　　Beneath Saint Peter's dome ;
And million, million, longing hearts,
　　Await the word of Rome.

VIII.

Well may his beaming eye grow dim,
　　His tongue refuse to speak ;
The blood rush back quick to his heart,
　　And leave all pale his cheek.
A thousand lives with all their joys,
　　With all their hopes and fears,
Are thronging in his bosom now,
　　And gushing in his tears.

IX.

A moment more, and he is calm ;
　　Then rings that wond'rous voice
Through Peter's dome, and spacious aisles,
　　To bid his sons rejoice.
A voice that thrills through every heart,
　　To tell of victory won,
That Mary's crown now shines *all* bright,
　　Its brightest gem set on.

X.

For, lo ! the mystic words are said,
  " Define,"—" Decree,"—" Confirm :"—*
To teach the world that she was free,
  Free, e'en from sin's sad germ
Nor lily fair, nor driven snow,
  Are half so pure as she ;
Oh ! "Tota pulchra es," sweet queen,
  Nec, macula in Te."†

XI.

Oh, joyous day ! Oh, day of bliss !
  Oh, day of endless fame !
To shed its ray, oh, Pontiff great !
  Around thy deathless name.
Recording angels write thy words,
  While prostrate nations raise
Their song of glad and burning love—
  The song of Mary's praise.

XII.

A moment's dread and awful pause,
  With hearts too full for speech—

* "Definimus,"—"Decretamus et Confirmamus "—the words of the definition.
† "Thou art all fair, and there is no spot in thee."

And, then, a shout of holy joy,
 That e'en to heaven may reach ;
And every bell in Rome rings out,
 To waft the news along ;
While spirits blest, in realms above,
 Repeat the joyous song.

  * * * * * *

XIII.

To every clime the tidings speed,
 To fill each heart with joy ;
To bless the old man and the maid,
 The matron and her boy.
And many a heavy heart grows light,
 And many a weeping eye
Gleams with the fire of other days,
 As flit the tidings by.

XIV.

Across the sea the glad news came,
 E'en to our own poor land,
And Mary's children gathered there,
 A small, but faithful band :
And careless of the scoffer's voice,
 They dare their voices raise,
And tune once more the silent harp,
 To sing their Mother's praise.

XV.

And as they sing, what burning thoughts
    Come rushing through each brain !
As England seems, indeed, to be
    " Old England," once again.
And memories of the times long past
    Are swelling in each breast,
Sweet memories of the bye-gone days,
    When Faith our island bless'd.

XVI.

They seem to see those noble souls,
    That brave and fearless band,
Who brought the grand old Faith of Rome
    Unto our heathen land ;
Who freed our nation from its chains,
    Set Britain's children free;
Who curved the haughty neck to Christ,
    And bent the stubborn knee.

XVII.

They see the day when Rome's great sons
    Come o'er the bounding wave,
And bring the cross to Britain's isle,
    A standard for the brave—

A solace for the broken heart—
    A glory for the free—
And lead our land in willing chains,
    O Rome, great Rome, to thee.

XVIII.

They come not in the pomp of pride,
    With mighty spear and sword;
Their coat of mail their own brave hearts,
    And the glory of their Lord.
Poor humble monks, in lowly guise,
    They land on Britain's shore,
And softly sing the Virgin's hymn,
    As the cross goes on before.

XIX.

The haughty king in savage state,
    His nation's court doth hold,
And frowning brows, and curling lips,
    The humble monks behold.—
Yet out they speak, with right good heart,
    With little show of fear;
For God's bright flame is in their breasts,
    His mighty aid is near.

XX.

From Rome we come, an humble band,
　But joyous news we bring,
Unto thy nation, and to thee,
　O great and mighty king!
We come to tell you of your God,
　To make you great and free;
Then haste to curve the willing neck,
　And bend the willing knee.

XXI.

With eager ear they list the tale,
　With eyes more keen and bright;
And soon the stubborn heart doth bend
　Before the God of might.
And king, and court, and nation, all,
　Quick bend the willing knee,
And raise, with glowing hearts, their hymn,
　O Lord of Hosts, to Thee!

XXII.

They see the day when Britain's sons,
　Were one in faith and love;
One faith, one altar, and one hope,
　In Him who reigns above.

When Peter's sway was gladly felt,
　　Through all the faithful land;
And king, and priest, and peasant, all,
　　Obey'd his dread command.

XXIII.

They see the day when Mary's name
　　Fell on each British ear,
" Familiar as a household word,"
　　Each sinking heart to cheer.
When on each spire, and through each field,
　　And o'er each church-yard sod,
The cross was seen, in goodly guise,
　　To raise men's hearts to God.

XXIV.

Well may they weep that clouds arose,
　　To dim this happy scene;
To make us grieve and sadly sigh,
　　For glories that have been.
To make us turn with heavy hearts,
　　From England of to-day;
And weep to love and prize her less,
　　Than England passed away.

XXV.

Well may they weep for ruined fanes,
    For mighty temples gone;
Weep for the lamp, whose soft red light
    For ever, ever shone.
Weep for the homes, the convent homes,
    Where weary men might die;
The homes where every son of toil,
    At last, might close his eye.

XXVI.

In those glad days, no workhouse gate
    Was open'd to the poor;
The poor man sought, with trusting step,
    The convent's sheltering door.
And there with gentle nuns to watch
    Around his dying bed;
Naught need he reck, his time had come,
    His space of exile sped.

XXVII.

And if, perchance, his course was run,
    He gladly went his way,
From realms of toil, from realms of pain,
    To realms of endless day

Nor in the ground, like some dead dog,
　　Whose service term is o'er,
They laid him—but the grand old cross
　　Was carried on before,

XXVIII.

And close behind, the vested priest
　　Would follow gently on,
To sing the Mass, to say the prayer,
　　To bless the brother gone.
With careful and with rev'rent hand,
　　They laid him in the sod ;
They plac'd the cross above his grave,
　　Then—left him with his God.

XXIX.

Well may they weep, that English hands
　　Should seek a brother's life,
Should, gloating, spill a brother's blood,
　　In mad sectarian strife.
But, oh ! that white-robed martyr band,
　　Is still our chiefest good ;
For England's Church shall rise once more.
　　From out her martyr's blood.

XXX.

For, yet, once more, in Britain's isle,
　Shall happy days be seen ;
And Britain be more faithful still
　Than Britain that hath been.
Augustine's prayer, sweet Mary's might,
　Shall beam upon our isle ;
And England, yet, in Rome's bright crown,
　An isle of saints shall smile.

XXXI.

Oh ! yet, once more, o'er England's fields,
　The glorious cross shall wave ;
The solace of the broken heart,
　The standard of the brave.
And yet, once more, from every tower,
　Sweet bells peal forth the chime,
That calls us from our earthly task,
　To greet the holy time.

XXXII.

Oh ! yet, once more, within each cot,
　And 'neath each palace dome,
The cross shall find, with rich and poor,
　A glad and welcome home.

c

And yet, once more, shall Mary's form
    Rejoice each weary gaze ;
And infant lips once more intone,
    The hymn of Mary's praise.

XXXIII.

Oh ! yet, once more, through fretted aisles
    The vested throng shall press ;
And saintly priest, with lifted hand,
    The kneeling crowd shall bless.
And yet, once more, shall prostrate forms
    In busy streets be seen ;
And scatter'd roses mark the path
    Where, He, the Lord hath been.

XXXIV.

It must be so ; for Mary's love
    Is beaming on us still—
The love that cheer'd our father's path,
    And lighten'd many an ill.
And thou art rearing still thy sons,
    To send them o'er the sea;
To lead our land once more, O Rome,
    Sweet mother, Rome, to thee.

XXXV.

Oh, isle of saints ! Oh, Mary's dower !
　　How long ere this shall be ?
When wilt thou rise, throw off thy chains,
　　And once again be free ?
When wilt thou drive dark error's form,
　　Back to her native night,
And give to sainted George once more,
　　His fond, his ancient right ?

XXXVI.

Then rise, O star of blessed truth !
　　And shed thy brightest rays ;
And give this bonny land of ours,
　　The Faith of ancient days.
Nor English hearts shall count the cost
　　That waits them in the fight ;
But, breast to breast, rush fearless on,
　　And, " GOD DEFEND THE RIGHT."

THE ASSUMPTION.

HO is this that cometh up from the desert, flowing with delights, leaning upon her beloved?

Who is she that cometh forth as the morning rising, fair as the moon, bright as the sun, terrible as an army set in array?

Come from Libanus, my spouse, come from Libanus, come; thou shalt be crowned from the top of Amana, from the top of Samir and Hermon, from the dens of the lions, from the mountains of the leopards.—*Canticle of Canticles.*

And so I was established in Sion, and in the holy city likewise I rested, and my power was in Jerusalem, and I took root in an honourable people, and in the portion of my God his inheritance, and my abode is in the full assembly of the saints.

I was exalted like a cedar in Libanus, and as a cypress-tree on Mount Sion. I was exalted like a palm-tree in Cades, and as a rose plant in Jericho.— *Ecclesiasticus.*

THE ASSUMPTION.

Assumpta est Maria in cœlum ; gaudent angeli, laudantes benedicunt Dominum.—*Roman Breviary.*

I.

WHAT mean those sounds of joyous mirth that
    peal along the sky,
That seem to rend, so full and deep, the vault of
    heaven high ?
They roll along the boundless space where angels find
    their home,
Nor sweeter notes were ever heard beneath that azure
    dome.

II.

Anon they softly float along with such a witching swell,
That angel lips and angel tongues their raptures scarce
    may tell,
For harp and lute, and merry lyre, all swell the angelic
    strain,
And those who hear those notes of love may ne'er
    know grief again.

III.

And not alone doth music's charms delight that happy
throng,
But every joy that heart may feel is added to the song,
For incense sweet and richest flowers ambrosial fragrance shed,
And golden crowns, and rubies rich, adorn each sainted
head.

*　　*　　*　　*　　*　　*

IV.

But now on glad and lightsome wing they leave the
upper sky,
And wend their way as if to meet some one who
passeth by;
But as they rush in eager haste their heavenward path
along,
Again they strike the sounding lyre, again intone
their song.

V.

She comes, she comes, our Holy Queen,
She comes, the pure, the bright;
She comes in robes of glory clad
Amidst a world of light.

Then hail, O Queen ! with fondest love
 We kiss thy sacred feet ;
We strike the lyre, intone the hymn,
 Our lovely Queen to greet.

 ✦ ✳ ✳ ✳ ✳

VI.

And lo, SHE comes ! that spotless one, that fairest of
 Eve's race,
Within whose breast the stain of sin hath never left its
 trace ;
She comes once more to join her Son,—her sole, her
 only joy,
To greet as God, Him whom she knew a poor and
 helpless boy.

VII.

Nor angels thronging round her feet, nor seraphs at
 her beck,
Nor music sweet, nor treasures rich, her onward path
 may check ;
She casts no glance upon the scene, but upward still
 she hies,
With many a bright and joyous band, triumphant
 through the skies.

VIII.

Not e'en the chaunt of music sweet, the scent of richest
    flowers,
The charms of Heaven itself spread out, the homage
    of its powers,
Nor cherubim, nor seraphim, nor all the hosts above,
May for a moment stay her path,—a mother and her
    love.

IX.

She seeketh not those treasures sweet, though rich
    and rare they be,
She listeth not that swelling hymn, though high its
    minstrelsy;
Nor may they all, though great they be, her lightest
    thought employ,
Who seeketh Him who made THEM all,—her own, her
    only joy.

X.

And now they meet, those holy ones, that Mother and
    that Son,
The one to claim, the other give, the meed of glory
    won;
And all in vain she casts herself in rapture at His feet,
For 'tis not thus that such a Son a Mother fond may
    greet.

XI.

Her hand in His, her gentle head reclining on His breast,
Mid shouts of joy and heavenly song she enters on her
    rest;
His loving voice its sweetest balm is pouring in her ear,
With all the love that such a Son may give a Mother
    dear.

XII.

A crown of stars about her head, a sceptre in her grasp,
A robe of glory round her form which richest jewels
    clasp,
With angels scattering at her feet whate'er is great
    and rare,
She enters thus her endless home, its endless love to
    share.

XIII.

And pause we here, nor vainly seek what mortal ne'er
    may know,
For angel tongues themselves may scarce her wondrous
    glory show;
A seraph's lips may scarcely tell the measure of that
    love,
Which she, the pure and spotless one, receives in
    worlds above.

XIV.

But yet, thou sweet and holy one, thou treasure of the
      blest,
Thou art our own dear Mother still, our refuge and
      our rest ;
Then cast an eye of love on us, poor exiles, as we roam,
And bring us in thy own good time unto thy own
      sweet home.

———————

THE
PRAYER OF ST. PATRICK.

THE PRAYER OF ST. PATRICK.

THE miraculous events to which I have alluded in this poem, are related on the authority of Nennius, Elv Probus (Vita Patricii). St. Fiech (Hymn), Jocelyn (Vita Patricii), and other distinguished early writers. I have used the "poetical license" in one or two instances, in regard to the order of time; but the *facts* adduced, are all to be found in one or other of the writers alluded to. Both Nennius and Probus give an account of St. Patrick's celebrated prayer for his people; made at a time when he had ascended the heights of Mount Cruachan-Eli in order to contemplate, bless, and crown his glorious work. At this period, after thirty years unremitting toil, all Ireland had been subdued, and reduced to the yoke of Christ. St. Patrick had founded three hundred and sixty-five churches, consecrated three hundred and sixty-five bishops, and ordained three thousand priests. Not satisfied, however, with all this, the saint now poured out his soul, as it were, in one torrent of love, praying God to bestow upon his dear children the extraordinary favours mentioned in this poem.

D

Great as were these favours—one of them, indeed,
placing St. Patrick in the rank of the apostles to whom
it was said: "You shall sit on twelve thrones, to
judge the twelve tribes of Israel,"—he, nevertheless,
obtained his requests; for, a little before his death,
an angel was sent to him to assure him that nothing
had been refused to him, and that he might be at rest
as to the future destinies of the people so dear to him.

To the efficacy of St. Patrick's prayer, who shall
say how much of Ireland's faithful long-suffering is to
be ascribed?   I trust that this simple poem may serve
to remind many a son of St. Patrick of the never-
dying love of his glorious patron, and to draw closer
and closer still the sacred cord which, binding the
father and his children together in a holy bond of
union, may be in all the coming years, as it has ever
been during those which are gone, the strongest and
surest stay of the children of Erin against every
attack which may be made upon the priceless jewel
of their Faith.   No matter whence that attack may
come, so long as his children "prize their Father's
name," they may surely live in the certain hope of
being united to him "beyond the glowing sky."

THE PRAYER OF ST. PATRICK.

I.

FAR in the western ocean
  There is a fair green isle,
Upon whose fields the face of God
  Doth ever seem to smile.
Her sons are true and fearless,
  Her daughters chaste and pure,
In this fair isle, 'gainst every shock,
  God's faith stands strong and sure.

II.

This isle (in bygone ages)
  Which shineth now so bright,
And spreads abroad, through many a land,
  The blessing of the light,
Herself was all in darkness,
  Nor light, nor grace had she
To raise her hands to God above,
  To bend to God her knee.

III.

For Druids held her captive
    By wile and magic art,
And turned away from God her Lord
    The beatings of her heart;
And deadened all the pulses
    That throbbed within her frame,
Nor throbbed, alas, to greet with love
    Her Maker's holy name.

IV.

But the day star rose upon her,
    With bright and cheering ray,
The star of Truth, to lead her on
    In God's own chosen way;
And Egli, Mel, and Locri,
    With trembling accents tell,
The advent of the mightier power,
    The conqueror of hell.

V.

Saint Patrick came amongst them
    With crozier in his hand;
And Druid Priest, and Pagan King
    Were banished from the land.

For king, and priest, and people,
　His mission all confess,
And raise to God one swelling song,
　His saving name to bless.

VI.

Of churches built and founded,
　Of Druids swept away,
Of Patrick's zeal, of Patrick's fruit,
　'Tis none of mine to say ;
For you, yourselves, may see them,
　All through his faithful land,
And read in page by ages writ,
　The work of Patrick's hand.

VII.

But, all his toil was over,
　And dim the old man's eye,
As with a glad and willing heart
　He laid him down to die ;
Lay down in all the fulness
　Of his merits, and his grace,
But waiting till the message came,
　To see his master's face.

L.

VIII.

I ween that priests and bishops
  Came hasting to his side,
To look once more on him they deem
  Their glory and their pride,
Their Ruler and their Master,
  Their Father and their Friend ;
To cheer with words of tender love,
  His passage to the end.

IX.

And gently round about him,
  Each one doth take his stand,
To note upon the old man's form,
  The mark of God's right hand.
The light of God, most surely,
  Is shining on him now,
And lighting up his pallid face,
  And beaming on his brow.

X.

And, he, the dying Patriarch,
  Well may his face grow bright,
Well may his paling eye blaze up
  With God's unfading light.

As 'fore his glazing vision,
  The thoughts keep flitting on,
Of mighty works for Jesus done,
  Of mighty conquests won.

XL.

And Erin's faithful service
  Is all before his sight,
Her duty, and her constant love,
  Her courage in the fight.
With the vision of her conflicts,
  Of her sorrows and her tears,
Of good fights, for the old faith fought
  In all the coming years.

XII.

And ere he passeth onward,
  To the dwelling of his love,
Once more he lifts his feeble hand
  To God, who reigns above.
Once more, on fair, green Erin,
  The island of his care,
The dying Saint doth raise his voice
  To God, in humble prayer.

XIII.

Four favours prays he for her,
    And prays with all his might,
With the light of God about him,
    In the silence of the night:
With his children crowding round him,
    To hear what he may say,
To catch the words their Father speaks,
    As passeth he away.

XIV.

And, first, he prays his Maker:
    That Erin's every son,
Who, 'fore his God, shall humbly weep,
    And wail for evils done,
Shall grace, and fullest mercy,
    E'en at his dying day,
In measure rich, from God receive,
    To wash his stains away.

XV.

And, still again, he prays him:
    Nor foe, nor stranger hand,
Shall hold for ever and for aye,
    Sweet Erin's fertile land ;

Nor by her sparkling rivers,
  Shall stranger's face be seen,
Nor stranger's foot, FOR EVER tread
  Upon her meadows green.

XVI.

Then, as the father's feeling
  Grows stronger in him still,
His voice doth rise more earnest yet,
  To shield his sons from ill.
He prays that Erin's children,
  Their Father's name may prize,
And, prizing, meet him face to face,
  Above the glowing skies.

XVII.

And yet, once more he prayeth :
  That, on the fearful day,
When, with fierce wrack, the earth and sky
  Shall, melting, pass away :
When men's hearts sink within them,
  Shall Patrick's form appear,
To judge his sons— Oh ! wondrous sight—
  Their trembling souls to cheer !

XVIII.

And, then, the old man falleth
  Back on his lowly bed,
Amid the tears of those who deem
  The holy spirit fled.
But, yet, again he speaketh,
  In accent's full of love,
And tells them of a message sent
  To him, from God above.

XIX.

And, how, that God hath promised
  To grant him all his prayer,
To watch, with never-sleeping eye,
  The island of his care ;
To guard her in her sorrow,
  To bless her in her joy,
To bless the old man and the maid,
  The matron and her boy.

XX.

To bless her with a blessing,
  That shall for aye endure,
Shall keep her sons still brave and true,
  Her daughters chaste and pure ;

Shall keep " the lamp" still burning,
 In spite of fire and sword,
In spite of stranger in the land,
 In spite of stranger lord.

XXI.

And then the old man laid him
 Right meekly down to die,
With folded hands upon his breast,
 And gladness in his eye ;
And glory shining round him,
 And brightness on his brow—
Nor surer seal of God's right hand,
 Was ever seen, I trow.

XXII.

And with what love they wrapped him
 Up, in the winding sheet,
By Bridget's holy hand prepared,
 And knelt around his feet ;
While angels hover'd o'er him,
 With chaunts and hymns divine—
Would, surely, need some loftier pen,
 Than this poor pen of mine.

XXIII.

Nor would I dare to tell you
　　How, for twelve nights and days,
The glorious sun kept shining on,
　　With never-setting rays ;
Till all the rites were finished,
　　Which loving care might pay ;—
Nor human pen, nor human tongue,
　　The wondrous tale may say.

XXIV.

Yet, may I surely tell thee,
　　O, friend and brother mine !
How Patrick's love, for aye, doth watch
　　O'er this fair land of thine ;
And, how the love of Patrick
　　Doth keep and fend it still,
And guard it, with undying care,
　　From error's blasting ill.

XXV.

Though sword, and pest, and famine,
　　May scourge her to the core,
No blighting scourge of *error's* pest,
　　May rest upon her shore.

But, hand in hand for ever,
　As ocean surges free,
Still Erin's sons their voices lift,
　My mother, Rome, to thee!

XXVI.

Nor sword, nor pest, nor famine,
　May rend the triple chain,
That bound her sons through many a fight,
　Through many an hour of pain.
E'en as her own green shamrock,
　That sparkles on her sod,
And speaketh still of *Erin's Isle,*
　Of Patrick, and of God.

XXVII.

Yes, Erin, o'er thy meadows
　How many a storm hath swept,
How long thy sons have felt the chain,
　How long thy daughters wept!
And, how the galling bondage
　Hath eaten to thy soul,
And forced the tears, thou fain wouldst hide,
　To flow without control.

XXVIII.

And, yet, I see thee walking
　　With all thy virgin pride
Still shining fresh upon thy brow,
　　To deck thee like a bride.
And, still, I see thy children
　　Fall down before thy feet,
To kiss thy garment's very hem,
　　Thy queenly form to greet.

XXIX.

And then, the years of bondage
　　Are hidden from my sight,
As, still, I gaze upon thy form,
　　So peerless and so bright,
Till I forget the slaughter,
　　The sorrow, and the tear,
Which were thy lot, St. Patrick's church,
　　Through many a weary year.

XXX.

And I can scarce conceive it,
　　Nor tell how this may be,
Till, dear Saint Patrick, all my thoughts
　　Go rushing up to thee;

And, then, I learn the wonder,
  As, musing on thy prayer,
I thank my God that Erin's church
  Is still Saint Patrick's care.

———————

SAINT DOMINIC

AND THE

INSTITUTION OF THE HOLY ROSARY.

𝔄 𝔏𝔢𝔤𝔢𝔫𝔡 𝔬𝔣 𝔱𝔥𝔢 𝔗𝔴𝔢𝔩𝔣𝔱𝔥 ℭ𝔢𝔫𝔱𝔲𝔯𝔶.

E

AND

Ǥhe Institution of the Holy Rosary.

———◆———

ᵍℱ ROM Palladius's Lusaic History, from Sozomen, and many other old writers, it is evident that the ancient anchorets and others frequently counted the number of their prayers by little stones, grains, or other such marks.

Long before the time of St. Dominic, St. Albert of Crespin, Peter the Hermit, and other holy men, are mentioned as having taught such of the laity as were unable to read the Psalter, to recite a certain number of Our Fathers and Hail Marys, in place of each canonical hour of the Church-office; but it is almost universally admitted that we owe to the glorious St. Dominic the devotion of the Holy Rosary in its present form, which consists in reciting fifteen decades, or tens, of the Angelical Salutation, with one Our Father before each decade, in honour of the principal mysteries of the Incarnation, including two peculiar to the Blessed Virgin.

It is related at the time the heresy of the Albigenses was making such fearful havoc in the Church of God, that St. Dominic, who had lately founded his glorious order, was engaged in prayer, earnestly beseeching the Mother of God, whose special privilege it is to overthrow all heresies, to give him some means of counteracting the blasphemous assaults which were made by these heretics on the sublime doctrine of the Incarnation. He received an admonition to institute the devotion of the Holy Rosary, and to propagate it as widely as possible amongst all classes of the people, as the most powerful and efficacious bulwark against the attacks of the heretics. How faithfully he complied with the heavenly admonition, and with what success, there is no need of repeating in this place.

That the glorious St. Dominic was the institutor of the devotion of the Holy Rosary is affirmed by several popes in a great number of bulls and briefs. It is also proved by the constant tradition of the Dominican Order. Father Echard, in his collection of the writers of the Dominican Order, adduces several convincing proofs of the same truth. And this is confirmed by Malvenda (Annal. Ord. Prædic), Monelia, (Diss. de origine Rosarii, Romæ, an. 1725,) Benedict

XIV., and many other learned writers.   The legend which forms the subject of the following simple poem is related in the Roman Breviary (see the office for the first Sunday of October, or Rosary Sunday).

St. Pius V. instituted an annual commemoration, under the title of St. Mary de Victoria, in thanksgiving for the great victory gained at Lepanto, on the 7th of October, the first Sunday of the month, 1571. In 1573 Gregory VIII. changed this title into that of the Rosary.   He also granted an office of the same to all churches in which there was an altar bearing the title of our Lady of the Rosary.   In 1716, the Emperor Charles VI., having defeated the Turks near Temeswar, on the feast of our Lady of Nives, and those infidels having also raised the siege of Corcyra the same year, on the Octave of the Assumption, Clement XI. extended the festival of the Holy Rosary to the universal Church, ordering it to be celebrated on the first Sunday of October.   The devotion of the Holy Rosary, while it is the source of innumerable graces to all who perform it faithfully, has ever been most dear to every true child of Jesus and Mary.

I Dedicate this Poem,

WITH EVERY SENTIMENT OF RESPECT,

TO THE

SPIRITUAL CHILDREN

OF

The Glorious Saint Dominic,

AND

IN GRATEFUL REMEMBRANCE OF MANY ACTS OF KINDNESS
RECEIVED AT THEIR HANDS.

ST. DOMINIC AND THE HOLY ROSARY.

I.

THERE is a glorious legend
 Of the times now pass'd way,
Of the times when Faith was brighter
 Than it is in this our day—
When the hearts of men were keener,
 For the things that are above—
For the glory of their Master,
 And the Mother of His love.

II.

A darksome cloud had risen
 O'er the sweet and smiling earth,
And it fell upon the patriarch,
 And the infant at its birth.
As it hurried o'er the mountain,
 As it rushed through the glen,
It scattered wide its noxious tide,
 Among the sons of men.

III.

Error's form was stalking boldly
 In the light of God's own sun;
It was jibing and rejoicing
 For the evil it had done.
It stalked along in triumph,
 In the might of fire and sword;
It blighted with its poisoned breath
 The peasant and his lord.

IV.

The maiden and the matron
 Were blasted by its spell:
'Twould be a long and dreary tale
 Its evil deeds to tell;
For it gathered strength and vigour
 As it surged in haste along;
And its yells were sounding hoarsely
 O'er the gentle vesper song.

V.

A holy monk was praying
 In his lone and lowly cell,
His eye was resting fondly
 On a form he loved right well:—

Mary's image stood before him,
And his face was beaming bright,
As visions floated round him,
In the silence of the night.

VI.

He saw the wolf devouring
The shepherd and his sheep;
And his noble breast was panting,
And his eyes were fain to weep.
And the love that burned within him,
For the glory of his King,
Was all too great for human heart,
Too deep for human thing.

VII.

He prayed the Virgin Mother
To raise her mighty arm,
To scatter wide the impious herd,
And shield the flock from harm.
He prayed her for her glory,
And the glory of her child,
To chase away this hellish foe,
To still this tempest wild.

*　　*　　*　　*　　*

VIII.

A gentle light is floating
   Around him as he kneels,
And the gleamings of another world
   Within his breast he feels.
Soft music gently sounded
   Through his poor and humble cell,
And a vision—oh! how glorious!—
   Upon him softly fell.

IX.

A lady stood before him,
   And the beauty of her face
Was such as mortal might not claim,
   Too pure for human race.
And her garments fell around her,
   With a rich and dazzling glow;
Far brighter than the sunshine's beams,
   Far whiter than the snow.

X.

A gentle infant nestled
   On her pure and spotless breast,
And his little arm was round her,
   As he close unto her press'd.

And the light of God shone round them,
   As they stood in silence there;
As they smiled with loving favour
   On the hermit at his prayer.

XI.

He looked with burning wonder,
   And his face more ardent grew,
For well he kenned the glorious sight,
   The vision well he knew.
And quickly down upon the earth,
   With beating heart he fell,
Whilst the heavenly strains kept sounding through
   That poor and humble cell.

XII.

Then the lady touched him softly
   As he lay in holy fear,
And she bade him rise and gird his loins,
   And be of right good cheer.
For he should be the warrior,
   With neither spear nor sword,
To scatter wide this impious band,
   To rout this hellish horde.

XIII.

'Twas not by earthly weapon
   This work was to be done;
For not by sword, and not by spear,
   Are greatest conquests won.
And whilst he looked in wonder
   For the weapon of his might,
The Lady's form more beauteous grew,
   Her lovely face more bright.

XIV.

She smiled with heavenly meaning,
   As a chaplet forth she held;
And the hermit's heart grew lighter,
   As his weapon he beheld.
And his breast was almost bursting,
   As she taught him how to tell
The holy beads, whose potent might,
   Should rout the ranks of hell.

    *   *   *   *   •   *

XV.

The holy monk has issued
   From his lone and lowly cell,
And eager ears are listening,
   For the story he may tell.

Men see God's mark upon him,
  As eagerly he pleads,
And tells them of his wond'rous gift,
  The Holy Virgin's beads.

XVI.

Quick through the Church's kingdom
  The Holy practice spread,
And soon that error's hateful form,
  Was numbered with the dead.
For it fell away before it,
  As the mist before the sun;
And the preacher and his holy beads
  The glorious fight soon won.

XVII.

Still the Church's children ever,
  In their hours of grief and pain,
Unto that holy chaplet turn,
  Whose virtues still remain.
'Tis the weapon of their warfare,
  'Tis their armour in the fight;
And they love it as the ensign
  Of their spotless Mother bright.

THE

LEGEND OF SAINT EDWARD,

AND

THE IRISH CRIPPLE.

THE LEGEND OF SAINT EDWARD,

AND THE

IRISH CRIPPLE.

HE interesting legend which is the subject of this
poem, is related by William of Malmesbury, St.
Aëlred, Brompton, and several other old chroniclers.

During the time that St. Edward was living in exile
in Normandy, he made a vow to perform a pilgrimage
to St. Peter's tomb at Rome, if it pleased God to put
an end to the sufferings of his family. As soon as he
was fairly settled on his throne, he began to take all
due measures for the fulfilment of this vow, urged on,
as he was, by his extraordinary devotion to the Prince
of the Apostles. Having summoned a great council
of his nobles, he laid before them the vow which he
had taken, and spoke of his great anxiety for its fulfilment. They (considering the as yet unsettled state
of his kingdom), while they highly praised him for his
pious intentions, still, most earnestly besought him not
to think of leaving the realm. The king, moved by

their entreaties, consented to refer the matter to Rome, and Aëlred, Archbishop of York, and Herman, Bishop of Winchester, were despatched to that city to lay the matter before Leo IX., who then sat in the chair of St. Peter. His Holiness, having taken the matter into consideration, dispensed with the king's vow, on condition that he should give to the poor the money which he would have expended in the expedition; and that he should, moreover, build, or repair and endow a monastery in honour of St. Peter. His Holiness was probably influenced in the imposition of this latter condition by his knowledge of the king's extraordinary devotion to the Prince of the Apostles. At all events, it was one which was most grateful to St. Edward.

After due deliberation as to the site of the new abbey, Edward pitched upon a spot called Thorney, where a small monastery already existed. Sulcard asserts that this monastery was first built by Sebert, king of the East Angles, on his conversion: but of this there seems some doubt. This monastery is first mentioned in 785, in a charter by king Offa. It was afterwards destroyed by the Danes, and partially restored by king Edgar. St. Edward, having fixed upon it as the site of his new abbey, repaired and endowed the old monastery in the most costly and magnificent manner, and, on account of its situation, gave it the name of Westminster. Pope Nicholas II., in a brief, dated 1059, conceded to it the most ample exemptions and privileges.

It was whilst residing in a palace near this church, in order that he might personally watch over the progress of the new buildings, that the incident related in this poem occurred. The consecration of the new church was performed with the greatest solemnity on the festival of Christmas; and it was whilst assisting at this great ceremony, to which he had looked forward so anxiously, that the holy king was seized with his last sickness. He died, in sentiments of the most heroic piety, on the 5th of January, 1066, in the 64th year of his age.

These are the facts which I have endeavoured to weave together in this simple poem. For several of the minor incidents, I am indebted to the beautiful volume of "Catholic Legends and Stories," in prose, published by Messrs. Burns and Lambert, London.

St. Edward was canonized by Alexander III. in 1161. In 1163 his body, which was found incorrupt, was solemnly translated by St. Thomas of Canterbury, in presence of Henry II. and his nobles, on the 13th of October, on which day his festival is now celebrated.

THE

LEGEND OF EDWARD THE CONFESSOR,

AND

THE CRIPPLE.

——◆——

I.

In the days when good King Edward
  Held in his royal hand
The sceptre of fair England's isle,
  And ruled a willing land ;
A strange and wondrous story
  Was passed from man to man—
A tale to fill men's minds with dread,
  And thus that story ran :—

II.

One bright September morning,
  Around the palace door,
A mighty crowd had gathered them
  Of nobles and of poor :
The Saxon and the Norman,
  Were there in gallant show ;
Such goodly sights we seldom see
  In England, now, I trow.

III.

But the Saxon brows were clouded,
  To see the stranger band;
For Saxon little loved, I ween,
  The Norman in his land;
While the Norman view'd the Saxon
  With a proud and haughty eye,
As they throng'd around the palace gate,
  To see the King pass by.

IV.

Out spake a Norman dandy,
  And bitter was his sneer:
What, ho! Sir Saxon Knights, he cried,
  What doth this reptile here?
Have you no choicer treasure
  To greet your monarch's sight
Than a foul and loathsome leper,
  Who festers in the light?

V.

The Saxons looked around them,
  With fierce and angry glare;
And Saxon hands were on sword hilts,
  And Saxon blades were bare.

But the Norman smil'd more proudly,
   And only waved his hand
To where, with still more eager press,
   The poor had ta'en their stand.

VI.

And there, upon the very step,
   Close to the palace door,
A loathsome thing had laid him down,
   A cripple, foul and poor.
His limbs were cramped and useless,
   Nor force, nor strength had he ;
The human form, in very truth,
   In him you scarce might see.

VII.

While the Saxons gazed in anger
   Upon the cripple's form,
And the scowling brow began to show
   The gathering of the storm,
The palace gate flew open—
   From out its portals wide,
The chamberlain came pacing forth,
   With slow and stately stride.

VIII.

And first, upon the cripple
  He looked with angry eye:—
What means this foolery?   Quick, begone,
  The king is passing by—
Nor, surely, on his palace step
  His eye shall fall on thee!
Quick, bear him off!   What, ho! the king!
  Down, nobles, on your knee!

IX.

The cripple prayed him sorely,
  And by his Maker's name,
To leave him where the king might look
  Upon his wasted frame:
From Rome itself, he pleaded,
  A message do I bring;
That message I, this very day,
  Must give unto the king.

X.

The Saxons scarcely listened—
  Well might the cripple pray,
As they seized him with unloving hand
  To clear him from the way;

And all was in confusion,
And naught but strife to see,
When, lo! the cry—the king! the king!
Down, subjects, on your knee!

XI.

And, lo! the good king Edward,
Hath stepped from out his door,
And, first of all, his glance, I wot,
Was cast upon the poor.
With stately grace he greeted
The nobles of his land;
But round his door, he most did love
To see the poor ones stand.

XII.

His step, so calm and kingly,
Doth fit him well, I trow;
And well doth England's crown beseem
His calm, majestic brow,—
And none shall tell the grandeur
That shone upon his face,
And made the Saxons prize so much
Its beauty and its grace.

XIII.

The Saxons loved king Edward,
   They loved his face to see;
Quick, Saxon knight, and Norman, too,
   Were down on bended knee:
But they looked with awe upon him,
   On the beauty of his brow,
And whispered that his time was short,
   That God was with him *now*.

XIV.

For it had gone amongst them
   His time was drawing nigh;
And well, I ween, they heard the news
   With weeping and with sigh.
And they prized him yet more dearly
   For the shortness of the space
They still might keep his royal form,
   So full of heavenly grace.

XV.

The king was scarce amongst them
   Ere he heard the cripple's cry;
And quick his royal glance had caught
   The cripple's longing eye:

Nor heeded he the chamberlain,
   Nor listened to his tale;
For, 'gainst them all, the cripple's cry
   Did with the king prevail.

XVI.

He stooped him to the cripple,
   And took him by the hand:
" Why, Muradoc, my own poor child,
   Thou'rt welcome to my land.
They told me thou wert praying
   At Peter's holy shrine.
What seekest thou on English soil,
   Or what of me and mine?"

XVII.

The cripple gazed upon him,
   And dragged him to his feet;
And looked into the mild blue eyes
   That did his glances meet;
Nor Saxon knight, nor Norman
   Might stay him speaking now,
Nor turn away the looks he cast
   Upon the monarch's brow.

XVIII.

" My good and gracious master,
     A message do I bring,
From Peter's shrine, from Peter's self,
     To England's holy king.
Five times I've dragged me weary,
     To ask of Peter's care,
To free me from my heavy cross,
     To listen to my prayer.

XIX.

" And hearken, king, I pray thee:
     For, what I now endure,
And all my ills, doth Peter say,
     Shall find a speedy cure,
When on his back, great England's king
     My crippled form shall take,
And bear me to yon altar's foot,
     For God and Peter's sake."

XX.

When the nobles heard him speaking,
     I wot, they raised a shout;
And pressing round him, fiercely sought
     To drive the cripple out.

But the good king waved them backwards,
    And raised his tearful eye,
And greeted with his bended head
    The message from on high.

XXI.

He stooped him down full lowly,
    To where the cripple lay:
What thoughts possess'd the lookers on,
    I scarce should dare to say,
As with his own right royal hands
    He raised him from the ground,
And round his own right royal neck
    The cripple's arms he wound.

XXII.

Then some did laugh out loudly,
    . And some did jeer and scoff,
To see proud England's noble king
    Thus bear a beggar off.
But their scoffs he little heeded,
    Nor aught that they might say,
As to Westminster's holy shrine
    He humbly took his way.

XXIII.

The king had scarce ten paces
　　His loathsome burthen borne,
Before the cripple in his limbs
　　Had felt new vigour born,
And all his joints were loosened,
　　His flesh grew clean and fair;
But still the king kept on his way,
　　Wrapped in his silent prayer.

XXIV.

The gazers saw the wonder,
　　And fearful grew each eye;
And down upon their knees they went,
　　To let the king pass by.
The laugher stayed his laughter,
　　And, prostrate on the sod,
The scoffers all were fain to fall,
　　And praise the living God.

XXV.

To the altar of Westminster
　　The king still sped his way;
Nor paused, until with careful hand
　　His burthen there he lay.

But his face was shining strangely,
  As he bade the cripple stand,
And walk abroad, that all might see
  The work of God's right hand.

XXVI.

The cripple stood before them,
  Nor any man might know
The loathsome and the hideous form
  In health's recovered glow.
And the hearts of all were swelling,
  As they gazed upon the sight;
Whilst many marked round Edward's brow
  A soft and wondrous light.

XXVII.

He knelt before the altar,
  For yet a little while;
And yet his face grew brighter still,
  With that unearthly smile.
My Lord, my God, my Master,
  They heard him softly say,
Of all thy gifts, I thank thee most
  For this, thy gift, to-day.

G

XXVIII.

His people pressed around him,
  And strove to kiss his feet,
And loving words from loving lips,
  King Edward well might greet.
But he heeded not their praises ;
  His face all crimson shone,
As passing out, he pointed up
  To God's eternal throne.

XXIX.

Three months had scarcely sped them,
  With fleeting haste along,
And Westminster's high vaulted roof
  Was ringing with the song,
As countless lips Te Deum sang,
  In one harmonious swell,
And countless hearts were raised to God,
  The tale of love to tell.

XXX.

For all the work was finished ;
  And it was one, I trow,
To fill all English hearts with pride,
  Make English faces glow

To look upon the abbey,
  So fresh, so fair, so grand—
E'en the abbey of Westminster,
  The glory of the land.

XXXI.

I wot that good King Edward,
  This consecration day,
Had waited with a longing heart;
  And now I scarce may say
What thoughts are burning in him,
  As louder swells the song,
As, through the fretted aisles, it peals
  Its solemn strains along.

XXXII.

But the holy rite is over,
  And his face is all alight,
As good King Edward strives once more
  To look upon the sight :
On the altar shining fairly,
  On the windows with their sheen,
And the fretted aisles, and vaulted roof—
  A goodly sight, I ween.

XXXIII.

The vested priests are waiting,
   The clergy and the lay,
Till good King Edward, from his seat,
   Shall take his royal way ;
And the long procession forming,
   Waits but the royal nod ;
But Edward's face grows strangely pale—
   His eyes are raised to God.

XXXIV.

One look he casts around him,
   Once more he strives to stand,
To clergy, knights, and nobles, all,
   Once more he waves his hand ;
And then the smile grows brighter,
   And brighter still his eye,
As e'en before that altar's foot,
   He lays him down to die.

XXXV.

What weeping and what wailing,
   What blanching of each face,
What hurrying out of eager feet,
   With hot and frantic pace;

With the moaning of his poor ones,
  Who had ever loved him well,
Is more than feeble pen like mine
  May now presume to tell.

XXXVI.

In the darkness of the winter,
  In its coldness and its gloom,
With heavy hearts they brought him,
  And laid him in his tomb:
In the shadow of the chancel,
  Where holy monks might pray,
They left him in the peace of God—
  He sleepeth there to-day.

XXXVII.

O'er the ashes of King Edward
  A glorious shrine they raise—
A shrine where Englishmen might kneel,
  And sing the song of praise:
For the memory of King Edward
  They cherished long, I trow;
Nay, at that shrine, but, all *by stealth*,
  You find them even now.

XXXVIII.

They have stripped the costly altar,
　　The shrine have pillaged too;
Oh, evil days, when English hands
　　Such evil work might do!
When the shrine of good King Edward
　　Was hack'd, and hew'd, and torn,
Oh, evil days! again I cry,
　　' When deeds like these were born!

XXXIX.

Yes, England, thou art mighty!
　　Thy sons are great in war;
Thy navies ride a thousand seas,
　　And bear thy flag afar.
But, of all thy boasted treasures,
　　No greater one is thine,
If thou did'st *know* it, than the spot
　　Where stands King Edward's shrine.

XL.

Thy monarchs, too, are mighty;
　　On their realms the setting sun
His shadow dark doth never cast,
　　As still he travels on.

But, are they half so mighty,
　Or half so grand to see,
As good King Edward bending him
　Down to the cripple's knee?

XLI.

Thy thoroughfares are crowded
　With many a busy throng;
Sometimes, to that old abbey, yet,
　There sweepeth it along
A coronation's pageant,
　With knight, and lord, and king,
'Mid shouts that make the abbey's nooks,
　With notes of welcome ring.

XLII.

But, very much I doubt me,
　If sight be ever seen,
One half so grand, as in that street
　In bye-gone days hath been;
When Edward bent him lowly
　Down on his royal knee,
And took the cripple on his back—
　A wondrous sight to see!

XLIII.

And bore him to the altar,
　　And laid him gently down,
And reck'd the cripple's new-born strength
　　More precious than his crown:
More precious than his jewels,
　　Or the sceptre in his hand;
A dearer gift to give to God,
　　Than England's fairest land.

XLIV.

But, spite of pillaged altar,
　　And spite of ruined shrine,
Oh, England! dear Saint Edward's fief!
　　Bright days shall yet be thine;
And English knees shall bend them,
　　And not, by stealth, at night,
But, with Te Deum swelling,
　　With altar blazing bright,
With countless thousands praying
　　Before Saint Edward's shrine,
And thanking God, for faith restored—
　　Oh, may this lot be mine!
If we this sight may witness,
　　Nor you, nor I, may say;
Yet, may we both Saint Edward beg,
　　To speed this happy day.

MISCELLANEOUS POEMS.

CHRISTMAS MEMORIES.

THE CHRISTMAS CHIME AND THE CHRISTMAS HYMN.

I.

LIST ! the Christmas Chime is pealing,
　With its ever-joyous swell ;
And the midnight sky is sounding,
　With the cheery ding, dong, bell !
From a thousand grey old turrets
　Rings the dear familiar chime ;
Ringing, ringing—bravely ringing—
　For the merry Christmas time.
From a thousand blazing altars,
　With soft clouds of incense dim,
Swelling, swelling, sweetly swelling,
　Riseth up the Christmas hymn !

*　　　*　　　*　　　*

II.

As out it bursts with clanging speed,
    Adown the frosty sky,
How many a ringing laugh grows still—
    How dim grows many an eye!
And how the long-pent love breaks out,
    The " Word made Flesh " to hail!
As ding, ding, dong, the Christmas peal
    Comes dancing on the gale!

III.

It telleth indeed of other days,
    And it sings of a by-gone time;
For ages have fled since first it shed
    The notes of its merry chime.
But tho' ages have fled, and countless dead
    Have bowed to the stroke of time,
Those stout old bells peal merrily on,
    As they ring the Christmas Chime.

IV.

It rusheth forth from its turret grey,
    With a sound right full and deep,
Like the wild wind's roar o'er the sea-girt shore,
    When it wakes from its summer sleep.

And it hurrieth out with a surging swell,
　And it seemeth in right hot speed,
For it knows that its song is a welcome one,
　And that love is its own sure meed.

V.

Yet it lingereth first in the old churchyard,
　And it whisp'reth round the graves,
With a mournful voice, like the babbling song
　Of the gentle summer waves.
It seemeth to wail, with its own sad notes,
　For the joys of the by-gone time !
It waileth for those who may listen no more
　To the song of the Christmas Chime!

VI.

Then away it hies through the midnight skies,
　And it floateth along the gale;
And it scattereth love, and it scattereth joy,
　As it danceth through the vale.
And it greeteth the young, and it greeteth the old,
　And it gladdeth each list'ning ear,
For it singeth this song—oh! a right merry one,
　But *once* in the passing year.

VII.

For those bells may sing, as they merrily ring
    To greet each Sabbath time ;
But they ring *this* peal but once in the year—
    At the merry Christmas time.
Then ding, ding, dong, as it rusheth along,
    It ringeth right merrily, oh !
And with ding, dong, bell, as it flits thro' the dell,
    It chimeth right cheerily, ho !

    *   *   *   *   *

VIII.

Then it hasteth away to a lowly priest,
    To tell of the Christmas time ;
And it knoweth of old how that holy man
    Doth love the Christmas Chime !
And he riseth up with a joyous face,
    And he donneth his priestly gear,
And he singeth the Mass of the Christmas time—
    The holiest of the year.

IX.

The altar blazeth with its lights,
    The incense burneth sweet,
The old faith's sons are kneeling now,
    The holy time to greet :

And the Christmas chime steals softly in
　To tell its joyous tale,
And it echoes the hymn they gladly sing,
　The Infant God to hail.

X.

And it seemeth loath to go away,
　And leave that altar bright,
For it fain would stay, with those who pray,
　All through the Christmas night.
It waileth for those happy days,
　When the land with faith was bright ;
When every church had its own sweet mass
　On the merry Christmas night.

　　*　　　*　　　*　　　*　　　*

XI.

But it hasteth on to a schoolboy's bed,
　And it whispereth in his ear;
And his cheek is flushed, and his smile is bright,
　As he murmureth "Mother, dear."
For he dreameth of home, and its wond'rous love,
　As he thinks of the Christmas time;
And his heart grows hot as he eagerly lists
　To the song of the brave old chime.

XII.

Then it scuddeth away for many a mile,
　On the wing of the wintry breeze;
And it beareth the song of the Christmas time
　To the wanderer on the seas.
And a hot tear steals o'er the sea-boy's cheek,
　As he clings to the rocking mast;
And a vision of love is bright in his heart,
　As he bends to the raging blast.
And he blesseth the wind as it burleth by,
　For it speaks of the Christmas time;
Yet his heart grows full, and his eye grows dim,
　At the sound of the distant chime.
For he thinketh, perchance, of his own dear home,
　Of the cottage so far away,
And the burning love of his mother's smile,
　That bless'd each Christmas day.

*　　*　　*　　*　　*

XIII.

I hear it now, that Christmas peal,
　And now the Christmas strain,
As angel tongues, with heav'n-born notes
　Thrill through me yet again;

And all my soul grows hot with love,
My eyes with tears grow dim,
As still I list from countless lips,
The holy Christmas Hymn.

XIV.

And list it now!—how softly sweet
It floats along the sky;
And now again, with gathering force,
Like voices from on high,
As on to Heaven the grand old hymn
Is wafted up above,
To mingle there with angel tongues,
One song of hope and love.

XV.

And who shall say its tones grow old,
Or who shall break the spell,
The Christmas Hymn for ever wakes
In hearts that love it well?
The scent of flowers is ever sweet,
The force of love e'er strong,
But fresher, brighter, stronger far,
The holy Christmas Song.

H

XVI.

It may be, voices now are hush'd,
 It may be, eyes are dim,
That once flash'd quick and bright to ours,
 To greet the Christmas Hymn.
And, as the first " Adeste" falls
 Upon the straining ear,
The sinking heart, the throbbing pulse,
 Tell of some lost one dear—
And for a moment we are sad,
 And scarce may sing our song,
As the Christmas Chime, and the Christmas Hymn,
 Float joyously along.

XVII.

An instant more, and it has gone—
 Our hearts grow full of love,
As a golden light comes gleaming down
 In brightness from above.
As cherished tongues are heard once more,
 The tongues of dear ones gone ;
E'en little children, praying still,
 " God bless us, every one."

XVIII.

On land, on sea, the Christmas Hymn
  Is still a welcome guest ;
It cometh like some angel glad,
  Or like some spirit blest.
Though sorrow's cup be brimming o'er,
  It wakes a mournful smile ;
It makes us think of happier days,
  And childhood's merry time.

XIX.

And, as the smiling spring-time sun
  Doth shed its beaming rays,
And speak of nought but blooming flowers,
  And merry joyous days :
E'en so, the holy Christmas Hymn,
  Doth speak of nought but love ;
And scattering fragrance o'er the past,
  Still points us to above.

XX.

And, still peal on, thou brave old chime,
  Go scatter peace and joy ;
Thou tellest of my father's love,
  His blessing on his boy—

My Mother's dear familiar smile,
And all the by-gone time ;
God speed thee, as thou hastest by,
Thou dear old Christmas Chime.

BALLAD.*

GOD BLESS US, EVERY ONE.

THE CHRISTMAS PRAYER OF TINY TIM.

" And so, as Tiny Tim observed, God bless us, every one."
From the *Christmas Carol.*—DICKENS.

I.

HE was a little feeble child,
And full of care and pain,
But yet with blithesome heart he sang
His simple Christmas strain.
God bless us all, cried Tiny Tim,
God bless us, every one;
So too we pray, this holy day,
God bless us, every one.

II.

They sat around their humble board
In Christmas mirth and glee;
In very truth, though low their lot,
A pleasant group to see.

* This ballad may be sung to the air of " The Soldier's Tear."

And Tiny Tim's poor pallid face
   With light and beauty shone,
As looking on them all, he cried,
   God bless us, every one.

III.

Another Christmas day came round,
   And Tiny Tim lay dead;
Yet as they deck'd his simple bier,
   They scarce could think him fled.
Upon them still the little face
   With kindly presence shone,
For still they seem'd to hear him pray,
   God bless us, every one.

IV.

Though many a place be vacant now,
   Though dim be many an eye,
Which erst would greet the Christmas chime,
   In gladness flitting by.
A golden light comes gleaming down
   From dear ones who are gone,
As pray we now with Tiny Tim,
   God bless us, every one.

CHRISTMAS SONG.

I.

LOVE thee right well, with the merry swell
　　Of thy brave old cheery voice;
As thou comest again, 'mid the hail and the rain,
　And biddest thy children rejoice.
I love the soft sheen of thy holly green,
　And I love on its leaves to gaze;
I love the glad sight of its berries bright,
　As they gleam in the yule-log's blaze.
　　I love thee, I love thee, I love thy brave chime,
　　I love thee right dearly, thou old Christmas time.

II.

I love thee right well, thou old Christmas bell,
　As thou swellest adown the vale;
I love thy sweet song, as it flitteth along,
　And telleth the Christmas tale.

Cold, cold is the heart that taketh no part
   In the joy of the Christmas time ;
That groweth not light, with glad visions and bright
   At the song of the Christmas chime.
      I love thee, I love thee, I love the brave chime
      That greeteth thee loudly, thou old Christmas time.

III.

I love thee right well for the tale thou dost tell
   Of days that are vanish'd and gone ;
When hearts true and dear met at least once a year
   Round the hearth, where thy gladness e'er shone,
Where the yule-log's soft gleam reflected each beam
   Of the eye, as we sat in its light ;
Where the tale and the song in mirth pass'd along,
   And looks in thy presence grew bright.
      I love thee, I love thee, and long for the chime
      That greeted thee bravely, thou old Christmas time.

IV.

I love thee, old bell, though a tale thou mayst tell
   Of hopes that are wither'd and dead ;
I bless thy glad peal, though its notes may reveal
   The absence of those who have fled.

Then linger awhile around yon old pile,
And murmur above their cold clay ;
I'll shed the hot tear o'er the lost ones so dear,
Then, joy with the friends of to-day.
Oh ! still do I love thee, and love thy brave chime,
And e'er will I love thee, thou old Christmas time.

LINES ON SISTER WINIFREDE;

A HOLY NUN,

WHO DIED WHILST ATTENDING THE SICK AND WOUNDED IN THE CRIMEA.

I.

THEY laid her in her lowly grave upon a foreign
strand,
Far from her own dear island home, far from her
native land ;
They bore her to her long last home amid the clash of
arms,
And the hymn they sang seemed sadly sweet amid
war's fierce alarms.

II.

They heeded not the cannon's roar, the rifle's deadly
shot,
But onward still they sadly went to gain that lowly
spot ;
And there, with many a fervent prayer, and many a
word of love,
They left her in her lowly grave, with a simple Cross
above.

III.

And yet she was a gentle soul, a timid, fearful thing,
Who, like a startled fawn, had sought her convent's
    shelt'ring wing—
Had left, with glad and bounding heart, a world she
    could not love,
And chosen for her own chaste Spouse, the Lamb of
    stainless love.

IV.

She thought to spend her peaceful days within those
    cloisters gray,
And with matin song and vesper hymn beguile her
    life away ;
She little thought again to roam amid the world's dark
    strife,
Save where sweet mercy led her steps to soothe the
    woes of life.

V.

Yet far away from her convent gray, and far from her
    lowly cell,
And far from the soft and silvery toll of the gentle
    convent bell;

And far from the home she loved so well, and far from
    her native sky,
'Mid the cannon's roar, on a hostile shore, she laid her
    down to die.

VI.

She loved full well her convent home, and loved its
    cloisters gray,
And loved full well those holy spots where she had
    knelt to pray;
Yet with a purer, deeper love, she loved the soldier
    brave,
And left her home, and left her all, his sinking soul
    to save.

VII.

She went not forth to gain applause, she sought not
    empty fame,
E'en those she tended might not know her history or
    her name;
No honours waited on her path, no flatt'ring voice was
    nigh,
For she only sought to toil in love, and, 'mid her toil,
    to die.

VIII.

E'en when the ruthless tyrant came, he found her
  brave at heart,
And struck her as she sought to heal the poison of his
  dart;
But he might not quench her holy love, nor dim her
  beaming eye,
And, joyous as a new-made bride, they saw her sweetly
  die.

IX.

They'll raise no trophy to her name, they'll rear no
  stately bust,
To tell the stranger where she rests, co-mingling with
  the dust ;
They'll leave her in her lonely grave, beneath that
  foreign sky,
Where she had taught them how to live, and taught
  them how to die.

X.

Yet might she claim one passing word, one token of
  regret,
'Twere fit that hot and scalding tears the soldier's
  cheek should wet,

For her who sought him in his pain amid the war of
strife,
And proved the deepness of her love—aye, proved it
with her life.

XL.

Oh, 'tis a fell and loathsome thing, this fierce sectarian
hate,
That thus would drag her noble deeds down from their
high estate ;
That thus can pass with silent lip those deeds of
wond'rous love,
Whose praise is sung by angel bands, in happier
climes above.

XII.

But oh ! she'll little heed their praise within her lowly
bed,
For spirits glad, around her grave, their choicest bless-
ings shed ;
Around her grave they softly flit on light and joyous
wing,
And gladly strike their golden harps, her well-earned
meed to sing.

XIII.

And whilst she sleeps beneath the Cross, which erst
    she loved so well,
Oh ! better far than bust or urn, *it* will her praises tell ;
'Twill tell her tale in glowing terms, give glory to her
    name,
And better far than mortal tongue, proclaim her deeds,
    her fame.

XIV.

The sweetest flowers that Nature yields shall bloom
    upon her grave,
The balmiest dews that Heaven can send that holy
    spot shall lave ;
And many a priest and many a nun shall raise their
    beaming eyes,
In joyous answer to the call, " *Go, thou, and do like-
wise.*"

LINES ON SISTER ELIZABETH;

Who died of typhus fever, whilst attending the sick and
wounded in the Crimea. She was buried by the side
of Sister Winifrede, and a simple cross marks their
last resting-place.

———

I.

IT was but yesterday we sang a sad and solemn lay,
O'er one who from this cold drear world had gladly
sped away;
Had ta'en her flight to happier climes, to realms of
bliss above,
To join, e'en in His own bright home, the chosen of
her love.

II.

Her funeral hymn had scarcely died in mournful notes
away,
No grass had grown, no flower had sprung, above her
silent clay;
When lo, once more those wailing strains fall sadly on
the ear,
To tell us of the opened grave, the sad funereal bier.

III.

Another spirit, pure and good, has gone her joyous way;
Another soul, 'mid duty stern, has breath'd her life
    away;
Has died upon that foreign shore, far from her own
    dear land,
Has found a poor and lowly grave upon that hostile
    strand.

IV.

It was but yesterday she saw her sister sweetly die,
And saw them lay her in her grave, beneath that
    stranger sky;
Yet as she softly turn'd away, she breath'd an ardent
    prayer,
That her own course might quickly speed—her resting-
    place be there.

V.

Her holy soul could prize full well the martyr's blessed
    lot,
Could prize above the monarch's throne that low and
    humble spot;
Could long, as holy souls can long, to gain their pro-
    mised rest,
To gain their true, their only home, the mansions of
    the blest.

I

VI.

She dropped a tear upon that grave, then gently went
    her way,
But her thoughts would wander back again, oft thro'
    the busy day;
And when her eye would sadly fall upon that lonely
    spot,
She *felt* it was her own last home, that grave her own
    sweet lot.

VII.

She did but bide His own good time, 'mid works of
    love and pain,
Her convent home, her native land, she ne'er might
    see again;
She knew full well the silver thread one single breath
    would sever,
And then, oh, love—and then, oh, bliss—her own
    chaste Spouse for EVER.

VIII.

And soon he came to claim his bride, his own, his
    spotless love;
And she trimmed her lamp, and gladly went unto her
    home above;

And once again that mournful hymn was wafted o'er
 the wave,
As they laid her by her sister's side, united in the
 grave.

.

IX.

She went not forth in youth's first flush, and when
 the step is light,
When Fancy fills the blithesome soul with many a
 vision bright;
For age had dimmed her beaming eye, and streaked
 her locks with gray,
When forth she went, with dauntless heart, to wear
 her life away.

X.

She left her home when home's sweet charms cling
 closest to the heart,
And when it wrings the inmost soul from that dear
 spot to part;
To leave, and that for evermore, the home we love so
 well,
To find the stranger's lowly grave in some forgotten
 dell.

XI.

Then honour rest upon her name, and glory be her
  meed,
Who thus went forth at duty's call, and in the hour of
  need;
Who thus could leave her convent home, ne'er to return again,
Whose woman's heart still bore her up amid those
  scenes of pain.

XII.

The merry bells are ringing now, and Peace is brightly
  smiling,
But yet our hearts cling round the spot where these
  pure souls are lying;
There is a memory round their graves, which tells a
  grander tale
Than all the peals with which glad bells proud Victory's
  advent hail.

XIII.

They sleep in silence, side by side, far from their own
  dear home ;
They rest not in the cloister's shade, nor 'neath the
  convent's dome ;

We may not kneel with beating hearts upon that lowly
    spot,
But oft our thoughts shall wander there, they shall not
    be forgot.

XIV.

Though pomp and pride may pass them by, and never
    breathe their name,
Oh! dear to *us* shall be their deeds, and dear their
    well-earned fame ;
And when our children gather round, and ask us of
    this war,
We'll lead them o'er the surging waves, to those low
    graves afar ;
And when each youthful heart is full, and dim each
    beaming eye,
We'll tell them how these noble souls went forth to
    droop and die :
We'll teach them that the brightest crown which Fame
    awards the brave,
Is theirs who sleep so humbly there, with the Cross
    above their grave.

AN OLD MAN'S MUSING.

I.

UPON a peg behind my door, there hangs an old
    black gown,
I never put it on me now—I seldom take it down ;
The dust lies thicker every day within its ample folds,
Yet few would guess how many a tale of bygone days
    it holds.

II.

My hair grows grayer every week—at least, my friends
    so say—
The youngsters whisper that I'm "slow"—"that I
    have had my day ;"
At every scene of sportive glee, with the "old folks"
    I am left,
As if my youthful days were gone—of life and mirth
    bereft.

III.

It *may* be so—it *may* be true—I may " have had my
    day;"
My vigour and my youthful strength may all have
    passed away,
And youth's bright hopes, before Time's scythe, have
    fallen withered down,
Yet all come back as I fondly gaze upon my College
    Gown.

IV.

My mother's proud and happy kiss upon my smooth
    young brow—
I feel it thrilling through my veins—I feel it even *now*;
No rush of care, no press of grief, the happy sight may
    drown,
My mother gazing on her boy as he dons his College
    Gown.

V.

My father's kind and manly grasp, I feel it on my
    hand,
As 'mid my peers, in college hall, I proudly take my
    stand,

With all my young heart's firm resolves to win a noble
    place,
To shun as death, whate'er *his* name may sully or dis-
    grace.

VI.

The friends of many a bygone year come crowding
    round me still,
And faces, cold in death's sad sleep, my soul with
    rapture fill;
Nor church-yard sod, nor seething wave, nor Afric's
    burning shore,
May hide the forms once truly lov'd, and lov'd for
    evermore.

VII.

My lonely room grows full of life, and visions from the
    tomb
Come flitting round me faster still, 'mid twilight's
    mystic gloom;
As gazing on that old black gown, past days return
    once more,
And friends long dead again repass dark Lethe's
    solemn shore.

VIII.

Another tale, a strange wild dream, my College Gown
    might tell—
Of one lov'd with a true heart's love—" not wisely,
    but too well ;"
Oh, faithless friend ! what fair bright hopes fell dead
    before that thrall !
But—let it pass—my College Gown may serve them
    for a pall.

IX.

I am an old and lonely man, but still my *heqrt* is
    young,
There's nought I love like the ringing laugh of child-
    hood's happy tongue ;
And, oh ! I'd like some childish hand to scatter o'er
    my bier
The incense that I most should prize—its sorrow and
    its tear.

X.

I'd like young hands to plant sweet flowers upon the
    church-yard sod,
When they have laid me to my sleep, in the peace and
    rest of God ;

I could not ask it *oft* I know, but in the twilight gloom,
I'd like young forms to kneel *sometimes*, and pray upon
   my tomb.

XI.

The hopes, the fears, of youthful days, in truth have
   passed away,
'Tis not for long—smile on me yet, "though I have
   had my day:"
Another day is coming fast—*then*, lay me gently down,
And wrap my poor old worn-out clay in my worn-out
   College Gown.

————————

MAY HYMN

TO THE EVER-BLESSED VIRGIN.

———◆———

I.

HAIL, holy Queen ! as once again
  Around thy shrine we bend,
And once again, with grateful hearts,
  Our grateful homage tend.
To thee, bright Queen, whose cheering love
  Lights up life's weary track,
Impels the just to noblest deeds,
  And wins the wand'rer back.

II.

Yes, once again before thy shrine,
  How gladly do we pray ;
How fondly press thy sacred feet,
  And weep to turn away :
For there we find that treasure sweet,
  That gift sent from above,
That never, never dying flame—
  A mother's ardent love.

III.

For we are thine, and thou art ours,
    Our best, our choicest gift,
To raise from earth our wand'ring thoughts,
    Our drooping hearts to lift
To that glad clime where thou dost reign,
    Amidst a world of light;
Where countless angels hail thee, Queen,
    The pure, the ever bright.

IV.

Then, holy Queen, our life, our hope,
    Our surest guiding star,
Look down upon our storm-tost bark,
    And aid us from afar.
And whilst the tempest roars around,
    Extend thy loving hand,
And bring us safe through dangers dread,
    Unto that " better land,"
Where troubles never dim the scene
    Of pure angelic joy,
Where spirits glad for ever find
    Sweet peace without alloy.
And bless us now, oh, Mother pure,
    Whilst thus we gladly twine
The cord that binds us to our hope,
    And makes us ever thine.

COLLEGE CHORUS.

GOOD NIGHT!

Air.—"The Hardy Norseman's House of Yore."

I.

OH! may we ne'er forget the hours, wherever we
    may be,

Which we have spent amid our friends, in gladness
and in glee:

The mem'ry of these happy days shall shine with
constant light,

Then, ere we part, sing every heart, good night, good
night, good night!

          [*The two last lines of each verse are repeated.*

II.

We'll ne'er forget our college home, wherever we
    may be,

Nor reck how far the distant land, how wide the
raging sea;

O'er many an hour of care and grief shall memory
shed her light :
Then, ere we part, sing every heart, good night, good
night, good night !

III.

No space can part the faithful heart, no matter where
we roam,
Or dim the never-fading light that gilds our college
home :
Then, once again we forge the chain, with friendship's
links so bright,
While, ere we part, sings every heart, good night,
good night, good night !

IV.

'Tis hard, perchance, to say farewell, and quit this
happy scene,
But coming labours shall be cheer'd by thoughts of
what hath been :
And part we now to meet once more, with hearts as
true and light,
Then, ere we part, cry every heart, good night, good
night, good night !

CYPRESS LEAVES.

NOT LOST, BUT GONE BEFORE.

I.

THEY bore him to that sunny clime,
  Where bright and cheering rays
For ever gild, with burnished gleams,
  The long and gladsome days.
Italia's beaming sky, they thought,
  Some healing balm might give—
Might summon back his fleeting breath,
  And bid their dear one live.

II.

For 'tis a land of life and love,
  In richest fragrance drest,
Which He who made this lower orb
  Above the others blest.
But when they saw him daily droop
  Beneath their watchful eye,
They brought him to his childhood's home,
  For there he wished to die.

K

III.

He sees once more his father's halls,
  And fondly looks around,
But ever and anon his eye
  Droops pensive to the ground;
For whilst he smiles he feels full well
  That nought on earth can save,
And sadly turning, softly marks
  His long, last home—his grave.

IV.

The merry spring again came round,
  And spread its treasures sweet,
But he was gone—we heard no more
  The echo of his feet.
So calm, so mild, he went his way—
  So trustful in his God—
We scarce could weep to lay his form
  Beneath the mossy sod.

V.

'Tis not the bright and sunny clime—
  The rich and glowing land—
That can, with all their boasted charms,
  Avert His chast'ning hand;

And when he takes the young and fair,
　Whose forms are seen no more,
We weep—why should we?—for " they are
　Not lost, but gone before."

VI.

They are not lost while Faith and Hope
　Can soar beyond the tomb,
Nor heed, amid the light above,
　Its darkness and its gloom.
They are not lost, while burning love
　May reach to Heaven's shore,
And travel back to murmur still,
　" Not lost, but gone before."

PASSING AWAY.

I.

THE world is passing from me,
  With all its hopes and fears ;
My soul is gently gliding
  From out this vale of tears.
A moment more of sorrow,
  A moment more of strife,
Ere the solemn message cometh,
  Ere I have done with life.

II.

The spring is smiling brightly,
  O'er the re-awakened earth ;
The daisy and the primrose sweet,
  Are springing into birth.
Each hedge looks gay and cheery,
  As it greets my glazing eye ;
Yet I hear the friends around me,
  In sorrow sadly sigh.

III.

I know not why they sorrow,
   I know not why they weep ;
Yet I feel their tears fall on me,
   As they gently bid me sleep.
Why do they look so sadly,
   And with such troubled gaze?
Perchance they muse on other times,
   And think of other days.

IV.

My heart is glad and happy,
   My soul is full of light ;
I hear soft voices singing,
   I see sweet visions bright.
I am longing to be with them—
   Those spirits pure and blest :
Then weep not for me, dear ones,
   I am passing to my rest.

V.

Spread sweet and fragrant blossoms
   O'er the bier on which I lie ;
Then bear me to the grey old church
   I lov'd in days gone by :

Sing the solemn Requiem o'er me,
　　Chaunt the Church's parting prayer;
Then place me in my long, last home,
　　And gently leave me there.

VI.

Plant flowers of joyous spring-time
　　Above my early tomb;
And sometimes come with loving care,
　　To mark them as they bloom:
Then as holy thoughts thrill through you,
　　Sweet visions of the bless'd,
Oh! pray for me, who pass'd away
　　In spring-time to my rest.

A DREAM OF THE NIGHT.

I.

ON a gentle summer evening,
    In a grey churchyard I stood,
With the rosy sun just setting
    All around me, in a flood
Of such bright and golden glory,
    As an angel's glance may greet,
On his heavenward pinions soaring;
    All the earth below his feet.

II.

But the stream of golden glory,
    Fading, fading, fades away,
And the evening shadows round me
    Gather with fantastic play:
But all through the growing twilight,
    Well-known forms keep flitting on;
Faces of fond friends departed,
    Visions of the dear ones gone.

III.

And my heart is wildly throbbing,
  With a strange and burning beat,
And the graves are heaving, heaving,
  In confusion at my feet.
And my boyhood's friends are round me,
  Boyhood's friends so fond, so true;
Whilst my tongue for ever waileth,
  Where, and yet, oh! where are you?

IV.

. Darker, darker grow the shadows,
  Deep'ning o'er the lowly sod,
Where a brave young heart is sleeping
  In the peace and rest of God.
Lo! his well-known face comes nearer:
  Feel I not the kindly hand!
Fly, ye shadows!—lighter, brighter,
  Glows the place on which we stand.

V.

'Tis my boyhood's friend is with me!
  Now, I strain him to my breast!
Ah! the cruel shadows deep'ning,
  Fall but on his place of rest.—

And my soul is longing sadly
    For the friend so fond, so true;
Whilst my tongue responsive waileth,
    Where, my boyhood's friends are you?

VI.

Deeper, deeper, grow the shadows,
    Where the sea-bird laves her wing,
And the waves, with ceaseless wailing,
    Still their solemn dirges sing
O'er a sad heart, sadly sleeping
    In the ocean's surging bed,
With no tongue to tell his praises,
    With no eye to weep him fled.

VII.

Deeper, deeper, O, ye shadows!
    Scarce a smile e'er cheer'd *his* way;
Scarce was there a heart to miss him,
    When his form had passed away.
'Neath the ocean wave now sleeping,
    None may know the sacred spot;
Yet *one* heart at least bewails him,
    Weeping o'er his hapless lot.

VIII.

Darker, darker, gather deeper
    O'er the dear ones who are fled!
Fall the hot tears quicker, quicker,
    In the presence of the dead.
None may take their vacant places,
    None this weary heart may cheer,
Which, in lonely sorrow waiting,
    Weareth out its exile here.

*   *   *   *   *

IX.

Lo! the darksome clouds dissolving,
    Lightly, lightly, flit away;
And the shadows, gently breaking,
    Herald the approaching day.
So, the wall of death and sorrow,
    Potent love shall rend in twain;
And fond hearts that here were parted,
    Shall, in Heaven, love again.

EVELÌNE;

A THREEFOLD VISION.

———◆———

I.

FIRST, a sportive child I saw her,
    Playing in her childish glee,
In the spring-time of her gladness,
    Playing round an old man's knee;
Looking with her eyes of brightness,
    Up into the loving face
That still gazed so fondly on her,
    On her beauty and her grace.

II.

As I marked her smile so peerless,
    Flashing, like the sunbeam's ray
Spreading sweetest fragrance round it
    On the blushing, new-born day,
All my soul expanded to her,
    To the gentle Eveline,
With a strange and wistful longing
    Wishing she were child of mine.

III.

Then her laughing face she nestled
    On the old man's loving breast;
As with childish pastimes wearied,
    Sank she gently to her rest.
With the old man's arms about her,
    Shielding still his gentle dove;
Watching, in the fond heart's fullness,
    O'er the treasure of his love.

IV.

Gazed I still and still more wistful,
    On the cherub at her rest;
And my soul grew full of envy,
    As she slept upon his breast;
In the confidence of childhood,
    Clinging to him closer still,
In his love protection seeking,
    From all danger and all ill.

V.

For I deemed that he was blessèd,
    Blessèd e'en as few may be;
Blessèd with a young heart's fondness,
    With its gambols and its glee;

With a faithful heart to cheer him,
 In his sadness and his gloom,
Flowers of fond affection strewing,
 O'er his passage to the tomb.

 *   *   *   *   *

VI.

Standing, once again I saw her,
 'Fore the altar's sacred shrine,
Looking, in her bridal garments,
 Almost like a thing divine;
With a modest blush just mantling
 Softly o'er her fair young face,
Shedding grace and beauty round her,
 Such as angel hands might trace.

VII.

Nought I wondered as I markèd
 How the old man sigh'd and wept,
How his fingers ever wandered
 To the place where she had slept:
Where her gentle head had nestled,
 In the sunny days gone by—
Days, when none but *he* might challenge
 All the glances of her eye.

VIII.

'Twas no wonder when he gave her
  To the brave youth by her side,
To the brave youth gazing on her
  With a husband's flashing pride,
That the old man wept more sadly,
  Though she clung about him still,
For *his* hands no more might guard her,
  Keep her safe from every ill.

IX.

Little reck'd he how she promised
  Still to prize him none the less,
Still to tend his failing footsteps,
  Still his constant love to bless.
To the stalwart youth he gave her,
  Gave the prize so fairly won,—
'Fore *them* shone the world all brightly,
  But for *him*, his task was done.

*   *   *   *   *

X.

Surely, yet again I saw her,
  In a still room, dark and drear,
Where, amid thick velvet hangings,
  Stood a black funereal bier.

Lighted by sad taper's glimmer,
    Strode I madly to its side,
Drawn by strangest fascination,
    Powerless to turn aside.

XI.

Long upon the sad sight gazed I,
    Well that stricken form I knew;
Deeper grew my fascination,
    Deeper still my sorrow grew,
Till, with fierce and bitter wailing,
    Sank I, weeping, by the side
Of the dear one I had cherished,
    More than all the world beside.

XII.

'Twas my fair one—but Death's finger
    With his seal had stamped her brow;
Thought I how I once had seen her,
    Thought I how I saw her now.
One short year's revolving circle
    Had too quickly sped away,
Since I prayed my God to bless her
    On her happy bridal day.

XIII.

And to think it—thus to see her,
　　Thus to hold her icy hand,
Thus to know that she has vanished,
　　Vanished, surely, from the land
Which such brief space she had trodden,
　　Like some spirit from above
Sent by God Himself, to teach us
　　Something of His own pure love.

XIV.

And to see the tiny infant,
　　Like a snowdrop, on her breast!
Sleeping—child and mother sleeping—
　　In the one eternal rest.
Sleeping in sad tapers' glimmer—
　　Sleeping free from care and pain—
Wondrous mystery!　Who shall clear it?
　　Give them to us once again?

XV.

Who shall stay that fearful wailing,
　　Who shall check the old man's cry,
From his hair release his fingers,
　　Or essay to wipe his eye:

Pour one drop of earthly comfort
　　On the old man's broken heart,
As he clingeth wildly to her,
　　Shrieking that they ne'er will part?

XVI.

Who shall stay the husband's anguish,
　　Who the swelling grief control,
Which, despising bound or measure,
　　Pierceth to his inmost soul;
Which (like fierce resistless surges,
　　Coursing madly to the shore)
Telleth of the strong man's anguish,
　　Weeping, weeping, evermore?

XVII.

'Tis the God, alone, who gave her,
　　Gave her but for some brief space,
Till the fire of earth might prove her
　　Worthy of the better place;—
He must soothe the old man's anguish,
　　Dry the husband's bitter tear,
Heal the broken hearts bewailing
　　Sadly round the funeral bier.

L

XVIII.

I, indeed, am but a stranger,
  Gazing on a solemn scene;
Musing in the heart's sad silence
  On the fair hopes that have been.
Musing on a sportive fairy—
  Musing on a fair young bride—
Keeping watch o'er child and mother
  Sleeping coldly side by side!

THE HARVEST MOON.

I.

SHINES the Harvest Moon full brightly,
 O'er the billows of the sea ;
Shines the Harvest Moon full softly
 O'er the upland and the lea.
Shines the Harvest Moon full queenly,·
 With her chaste and silver light,
With all nature sleeping gently
 In the silence of the night.

II.

Shone the Harvest Moon as brightly
 O'er the billows of the sea ;
Shone the Harvest Moon as softly
 O'er the upland and the lea.
Shone the Harvest Moon as queenly
 As she shineth even now,
Though her light, alas, was shining
 On a dying maiden's brow !

III.

Full of sorrow, watching sadly,
  As we stood about the bed ;
In the midnight silence thinking
  Of the spirit that had fled !
With the Harvest Moon bright shining,
  In her rich and silver sheen,
O'er the leaves of autumn falling,
  (Like the maiden that had been.)

IV.

Drooping slowly, slowly failing,
  Growing paler every day ;
We had watch'd our fair one flitting
  To her home of love away.
Through the spring, and through the summer,
  We had mark'd the paling eye ;
When the Harvest Moon was shining,
  Came the message from on high !

V.

Once again, so softly speaking,
  Once again we heard her say—
"Close about me, dear ones, standing,
  Watch my spirit flit away !

Let your voices whisper to me
  Words of hope and trusting love !
As my spirit passeth onward
  To its home of bliss above!"

VI.

Then her faint voice, fainter growing,
  (As her spirit ebb'd still more ;)
Like the distant surges breaking
  On the ocean's sounding shore.
With the angels she was speaking,
  And her face was all alight ;
Then we knew that God was with her,
  That her soul was full of light !

VII.

Then we watch'd the shadow creeping
  O'er her pale and fading face ;
Watch'd it stealing, surely stealing,
  All her beauty, light, and grace.
While the Harvest Moon came shining
  (As she shineth even now)
Through the casement—shining sadly
  On the dying maiden's brow !

VIII.

In the dead room, watching, watching,
    In the silence of the night;
With the calm face softly sleeping
    In the moonbeams' silver light.
With a sad heart, sadly thinking
    Of the sister that had fled;
With a sad heart, sadly weeping
    In the presence of the dead!

A BETTER WORLD THAN THIS.

I.

HASTE ! quickly pluck the cypress leaf,
    And toll the solemn knell,
Nor bid us check the wailing cry
    For dear ones loved too well.
But let us loose the strings of woe,
    Nor check the falling tear,
That springs from sorrow's faithful eye,
    To bless a lost one dear.
              Weep ! weep ! weep !

II.

As gentle flowers by summer heat
    Are nipped in their young bloom,
So do the loved ones of this earth
    Haste to the silent tomb.
The infant in its childish grace,
    The maiden in her prime,
Fall stark and dead, and flit away
    From out the realms of time.
              Wail ! wail ! wail !

III.

And many a heart that once was light,
   And strong in its young pride,
That stood as firm as some brave oak
   Upon the mountain's side,
Hath felt the lightning's withering flash,
   When all its glory fled,
And left it but a leafless thing,
   With branches sere and dead,
A sad memorial of the past,
   Of glory that hath been,
Of happy days and sunny hours
   Which loving hearts have seen:
For sorrow rends with savage hand,
   Each fond, each well-loved tie,
And leaves us oft one only wish,
   One only hope—to die.
            Toll! Toll! Toll!

*   *   *   *

IV.

Oh, this would be a dreary world,
   If all were ending *here;*
'Twould be a world of sighs and grief,
   With naught to soothe and cheer.

But lay aside the cypress wreath,
  Nor toll the solemn knell;
There is a happier land than this,
  For those we loved so well.
And cheer thee up, poor broken heart,
  And ease thy aching breast;
There is a better world than this,
  A home of peace and rest.
And wipe away thy scalding tears,
  And fill thy soul with love;
For God doth bind the broken reed,
  In realms of bliss above.
           Sing! sing! sing!

TRANSLATIONS.

TRANSLATIONS.

THE SACRED HEART OF JESUS.

Quicumque certum.

I.

Haste! all who, 'mid life's thorny ways,
　　Sure comfort seek, and peace, and rest;
Haste! all by burning care weigh'd down,
　　By sharp and bitter pain opprest.

II.

To Jesu haste, the spotless Lamb,
　　The Lamb by love for sinners slain,
Haste to his meek and wounded Heart,
　　The solace sweet for every pain.

III.

Oh! list those sweet and loving words,
　　His mercy list, his ardent call,
To me, poor weary wand'rers, haste,
　　Haste, all opprest by sin's dark thrall.

IV.

Oh! say what heart more sweet, more meek
    Than His who, nail'd unto the Cross,
Doth for his murd'rers mercy beg,
    To ward away their souls' sad loss.

V.

O Heart! the joy of heav'nly hosts,
    Of man the hope, the only stay,
Drawn by thy sweet and loving voice,
    To Thee we haste, and humbly pray.

VI.

Oh! free us from our sinful stains,
    And wash us in thy saving gore,
A new heart give to all who now
    With weeping eyes thy love implore.

ANOTHER HYMN FOR THE SAME.

𝔄uctor beate sæculi.

I.

Great Maker of the world's wide frame,
   All hail! our souls' redeeming Lord!
The Father's bright eternal flame,
   His sole, his uncreated Word.

II.

Thy bright and burning love Thee clad
   In Nature's weak and fragile clay,
That Thou to Nature might'st restore
   What the first Adam took away.

III.

That same pure ardent love did form
   The earth, the sea, the glowing stars:
Bewailing all our father's faults,
   Thou healest all our sinful scars.

IV.

Oh! in thy sweet and loving heart,
   Ne'er let this burning love decay;
But let this fountain still remain,
   To wash our sinful stains away.

V.

For this the lance thy heart did pierce,
　For this upon the Cross it bled,
That o'er our stains its mingled stream,
　It might, in loving plenty, shed.

VI.

To God the Father, and the Son,
　May brightest glory still remain;
Whilst equal power, and equal might,
　The Holy Spirit e'er doth claim.

THE NATIVITY OF OUR LORD.

Jesu Redemptor omnium.

I.

Jesu! our souls' redeeming Lord,
The God by loving hearts adored,
Who, ere the dawn of primal light,
Didst share in all the Father's might.

II.

Glad brightness of thy Father's rays,
The crowning hope of all our days,
Whilst through the world thy children bend,
Oh! to our lowly prayers attend.

III.

Remember, Lord, thou didst assume
Within thy stainless Mother's womb
Our mortal form, that, clad in flesh,
Thou mightst our sinking souls refresh.

IV.

As yearly comes this solemn day,
Glad homage all thy children pay,
Its tidings sweet they all confess,
And Thee, their sole Redeemer, bless.

V.

The heav'ns above, the rolling main,
And all that earth's wide realms contain,
With joyous voice now loudly sing,
The glory of their new-born King.

VI.

And we, too, ransomed by the tide
Which issued from thy sacred side,
On this thy Natal Day rejoice,
And homage pay with eager voice.

VII.

Jesu! to Thee, the Virgin's Son,
Be everlasting homage done,
To God the Father we repeat
The same, and to the Paraclete.

―――――

THE SACRED PASSION OF OUR LORD.

Pange, lingua, gloriosi.

I.

Sing, my tongue, with glowing accents,
   Of thy Saviour's death the strain;
Sing the great and noble triumph
   Of thy God by sinners slain:
How, upon the Cross triumphing,
   He for man did mercy gain.

II.

Grieving in his tender mercy
   O'er his fallen creatures' sin,
He, their woes to soothe and soften,
   Did in loving haste begin,
And the tree marked out, which later
   Should for sinners mercy win.

III.

Such the order of redemption
   By the Lord our God decreed,
O'er the wily serpent's projects,
   Thus in triumph to succeed;
That the fatal tree of Eden
   Man to glory bright should lead.

IV.

When the time of grace and mercy
   In its fulness had drawn nigh,
He, the world's Redeemer, coming
   From his Father's throne on high,
Clad in flesh of purest Virgin,
   Came to suffer and to die.

V.

See the new-born infant Jesus,
   In a lowly manger lie!
See his Mother's gentle fingers
   His poor humble garments tie!—
As with loving hand she swathes him
   List her fond maternal sigh!

VI.

Bright and everlasting glory
    To the sacred Triad be!
To the Father, Son, and Spirit,
    Equal glory ever be;
Heaven, earth, and all creation,
    Praise You ever, One in Three

ANOTHER HYMN OF THE SACRED PASSION.

Mœrentes oculi, spargite lacrymas.

I.

With sorrow deep oppress'd now let us sadly wail,
    And fill our very hearts with bitter grief and shame,
Whilst musing on the wounds, the pain, and torments
        dread,
        Which cruel man for God did frame.

II.

Behold the impious band with deadly haste draw nigh!
    See how with swords and staves upon the Lord they
        rush!
Then madly strike the Lamb, and then with savage
        blows
        That head divine they fiercely crush.

III.

But yet comes not the end: now bound with cruel cords,
   Unto the savage scourge the Lord of life they give;
And then without remorse, fierce ruffian hands are rais'd
     'Gainst Him who causeth all to live.

IV.

List! O ye people, list! the good and loving God
   In gentlest meekness stands beneath the lash severe;
And while his blood runs down, all guiltless though
    he be,
     No word he speaks his fame to clear.

V.

What man who would not weep? Not even yet the race
   Of sin, the viper's brood, their bitter hate have
    quench'd,
Upon his brow divine a thorny crown they press,
     And all his face with gore is drench'd,

VI.

Then—blackest, deadliest sin!—with rude and cutting
    cords
   They drag our loving Lord unto the place of death;
Upon the Cross he dies, and to his Father's care
     Resigns his soul with his last breath.

VII.

,To Him who freely died upon the bitter Cross,
　　To gain for sinful man sweet mercy, peace, and grace,
Be honor, fame, and praise—be glory ever sung,
　　In notes of joy by all our race.

PRAYER OF OUR LORD IN THE GARDEN.

Aspice ut Verbum Patris a supernis.

I.

Burning with mercy, from his throne eternal,
　　Bright in his glory, see the Word descend,
Bringing to mortals joy, and peace, and blessing,
　　　　　　　Never to end.

II.

Weeping in sorrow, man's sad loss deploring,
　　Eager to heal us, and to staunch our wound,
In his heart's anguish, as he prays he falleth
　　　　　　　To the cold ground.

III.

Bitter the sorrow which his heart oppresseth,
　　Wrapp'd in sad anguish ere the fight be won,
" Father," he crieth, as the cup he draineth,
　　　　　　" Thy will be done."

IV.

Fearful the anguish which then weigh'd upon him,
  As in his sorrow, he falleth on the ground :
Whilst the red shower, from each vein outpouring,
      Streameth around

V.

But from his Father, quick an Angel cometh,
  Gently to soothe him and assuage his pain,
And with new vigour, he to the dread conflict
      Turneth again.

VI.

Praise to the Father, glory dread attending
  Thee, great and mighty, His co-eternal Son ;
Praise to the Spirit in the highest heaven,
      While ages run.

THE MOST HOLY CROWN OF THORNS.

Exite, Sion filiæ

I.

Haste forth, O Sion's royal maids,
  Haste forth to see the gory crown
Which Sion's hands, with cruel skill,
  Have woven for her sinless Son.

II.

Those sharp and piercing briars, see!
  Which, 'mid his blood-stain'd locks, entwine,
Those pale and ghastly features view!
  Robbed of their beauty all divine.

III.

Oh! say what bleak and rugged earth
  Did those foul thorns so cruel bear?
Oh! say what stern and savage hand,
  Did weave them for his brow to wear?

IV.

But bright and fragrant glowing now,
  And ruddy with his saving gore,
Oh! brighter than all martyrs' crowns,
  Be those sharp thorns for evermore.

V.

Sweet Lord, the thorns which tore thy head,
 Were nourish'd by our guilt and sin;
Then from our hearts its thorns expel,
 And plant thy gentle love therein.

VL.

Glad blessing, honour, fame, and praise,
 Attend the Father, and the Son;
The Spirit equal glory crown,
 While endless days their course do run.

THE MOST HOLY SPEAR.

Quænam lingua tibi, O Lancea.

I.

What tongue shall give thee thanks, in fitting strains
 repeat
Thy praise, thrice holy Spear, on earth or up above,
Which openedst Christ's blest side, from whence the
  Church came forth,
 The living token of his love.

II.

When first the world was made, from Adam sunk in
    sleep,
    By God's all-mighty hand was Eve his helpmate
        form'd :—
From that co-mingled stream which from his side did
    flow,
    His Church, the second Adam form'd.

III.

Be equal praise to you, O high and blessed Nails,
    Which nail'd our gentle Lord unto the bitter tree ;
For his all-saving blood our doom of death effaced,
    And routing hell, made all men free.

IV.

Oh! may thy saints, sweet Lord, with deepest joy e'er
    praise
    That ever-burning love, which doth thy wounds
        retain
In that eternal clime, where with the Father, Thou,
    And Holy Ghost, doth ever reign.

THE MOST HOLY WINDING SHEET.

Gloriam sacræ celebremus omnes.

I.

With grateful voices, with anthems loudly swelling,
  Tell we the glories of our Lord's Winding Sheet,
Raise we the trophies of our hearts' devotion,
        His pure love to greet.

II.

O sacred object of our best affections!
  Bearing upon thee those marks of woe impress'd,
Which thou received'st, in thy folds enwrapping
        Our Redeemer blest.

III.

In thy sad presence bitter thoughts returning,
  Tell all the sorrows which our sweet Lord did bear,
Tell, too, his mercy, that the sons of Adam
        Might His glory share.

IV.

Painted on thee, too, his open'd side beholding,
  We, sadly weeping, his mangled members see,
His gory visage, his hands and feet so holy,
        Nailed to the tree.

V.

Surely no mortal, as this sight he vieweth,
   May, in his sorrow, the flowing tears control,
While sighs of anguish, deep and bitter, swelling,
               Rise within his soul.

VI.

O sweetest Jesu! 'twas my sin that slew Thee,
   'Twas my transgression that struck the cruel blow,
My life I owe Thee, gladly back I give Thee
               What Thou didst bestow.

VII.

Jesu, we praise Thee; glory bright attend Thee,
   Who didst redeem us by Thy all-saving gore,
Praise to thy Father, with the Spirit Blessed,
               Reigning for evermore.

3

THE MOST PRECIOUS BLOOD.

Festibis resonent compita bocibus.

I.

With glad and joyous strains now let each street re-
sound,
  And let the laurel wreath each Christian brow en-
  twine;
With torches waving bright, let old and young go forth,
  And swell the train in solemn line.

II.

Whilst we with bitter tears, with sighs and grief
  profound,
  Wail o'er the saving Blood, pour'd forth upon the
  tree,
Oh! deeply let us muse, and count the heavy price,
      Which Christ hath paid to make us free.

III.

The primal man of old, who fell by serpent's guile,
  Brought death and many woes upon his fallen race;
But our new Adam, Christ, fresh life unto us gave,
      And brought to all ne'er-ending grace.

IV.

To heaven's highest height, the wailing cry went up
  Of Him, who hung in pain, God's own eternal Son;
His saving, priceless blood, his Father's wrath ap-
    peased,
        And for his sons full pardon won.

V.

Whoe'er in that pure blood his guilty soul shall wash,
  Shall from his stains be freed—be made as roses
    bright—
Shall vie with Angels pure, shall please his King and
  Lord,
        And precious shine in his glad sight.

VI.

Oh! from the path of right ne'er let thy steps depart,
  But haste thee to the gaol in virtue's peaceful ways;
Thy God who reigns on high will e'er direct thy steps,
        And crown thy deeds with blissful days.

VII.

Father of all things made, to us propitious be,
  For whom thy own dear Son, his saving Blood did
    spill;
O Holy Spirit, grant, the souls by thee refreshed,
        Eternal bliss may ever fill.

THE ADORABLE SACRAMENT OF THE ALTAR.

Pange, lingua, gloriosi.

I.

Haste, my tongue, with glowing accents,
　Haste, thy Lord's high praise to sing,
Sing His Body's saving mystery,
　Sing the Blood of life's great King ;
Sing the Root of man's redemption,
　Which a fruitful womb did bring.

II.

Springing from a stainless Virgin,
　Born for man from realms above,
He with men on earth conversing,
　Sows the seeds of truth and love ;
Then with marks of deepest mercy,
　Seals his mission from above.

III.

At that last great Paschal banquet
　With his chosen band he eats ;
They the Paschal rites fulfilling,
　Spread the law's appointed meats,
Then the Food, all food excelling,
　All their wond'ring senses greets.

IV.

Word Incarnate! Man's Redemption!
    Bread into His flesh he turns;
Wine to saving Blood converting,
    (Though no sense with rapture burns,)
But the heart of trusting meekness
    Quick the sign of mercy learns.

V.

Wrapt in burning adoration
    Down before the Host we fall,
And all ancient rites resigning,
    Hail Thee, Jesu, Lord of all;
While for nature faith supplying,
    Bending low on thee we call.

VI.

To the Father, Great, Eternal,
    To his Co-Eternal Son,
To the Holy Ghost proceeding
    Forth from both, be honour done;
Equal glory, fame, and blessing,
    While all days their course do run,

GOD'S BRIGHT MOTHER, AVE!

Ave Maris Stella.

I.

God's bright Mother, Ave!
  Hail, O Virgin blest,
Star of ocean guiding
  To the port of rest.

II.

Whilst the Angel's Ave,
  Gladly we rehearse,
Peace unto us bringing,
  Eva's name reverse.

III.

Loose our sinful fetters,
  Evils drive away,
Light upon us shedding.
  Graces for us pray.

IV.

Oh, be thou our Mother,
  Take to him our love,
Who, for man's redemption
  Left his throne above.

N

v.

Purest of all Virgins,
  Cast thy mantle o'er us;
Sin's foul stains removing,
  Chaste and humble make us.

vi.

Crown our lives with virtue,
  Succour to us bring,
Till, with thee uniting,
  Jesu's praise we sing.

vii.

Praise and glory ever
  To the Father be,
To the Son, and Holy Ghost,
  One honour to the Three.

HELP OF CHRISTIANS

Sæpe dum Christi populus cruentis.

i.

Oft in dread danger, whilst the foe oppressing
  Hemm'd round in conflict the feeble Christian band,
Hath the great Virgin to its succour hasten'd
  From her bright land.

II.

Thus tell the trophies by our fathers raiséd;
   Thus too the temples which clad in spoils appear ;
Whilst joyous anthems, in her honour pealing,
       Gladden each year.

III.

But for new favours, Mary's praises singing,
   Raise we our voices in glad and joyous swell ;
Let all the universe, heart and voice uniting,
       Her praises tell.

IV.

Oh ! day of mercy, day of brightest bounty,
   When Faith's great ruler in joy returned again ;
Coming from exile, o'er his faithful people
       Gladly to reign.

V.

Haste! youths and virgins, priests and people, haste ye,
   And with loud anthems swell the sounding lay;
To Heav'n's bright Mistress, by your heart's devotion,
       Sweet homage pay.

VI.

Virgin of Virgins ! Jesu's Mother holy !
  In thy sweet mercy these favours still increase ;
Oh ! may our Pastor to bright joys conduct us
      Never to cease.

VII.

To the blest Trinity, praise and endless blessing,
  Might, power, and glory, may we for ever sing ;
May Heav'n's high mansions with our song of triumph
      Through ages ring.

THE DOLOURS OF THE BLESSED VIRGIN.

O quot undis lacrymarum.

I.

Oh ! what waves of deepest anguish
    On that gentle mother press,
As her mangled son she straineth
    In a mother's fond caress ;
As with weeping eyes she gazeth,
    And his gory form doth bless !

II.

With her bitter tears she batheth
  Then his mouth, and then his side,
Then those channels of redemption
  Whence did flow the saving tide;
All his sacred wounds embracing,
  In their mercy gaping wide.

III.

With a hundred, with a thousand
  Long embraces, fond and sweet,
On his pallid form she gazeth,
  Kissing all his wounds so deep;
Then worn out with grief and sorrow,
  Falleth fainting at his feet.

IV.

Sweetest Mother! lo! we pray thee,
  By thy own affliction sore,
By thy Son's last dying torments,
  By his streaming crimson gore,
Pierce our hearts with thine own sorrow,
  As thou didst his death deplore.

v.

To the everlasting Father,
　　To his ever blessed Son,
To the co-eternal Spirit,
　　Three in One, be homage done;
Be salvation, praise, and blessing,
　　While all days their course do run.

———————

PURITY OF THE BLESSED VIRGIN.

Præclara custos Virginum.

I.

Hail, guardian of the Virgin train,
Bright gate of Heaven's resplendent fane,
O peerless Mother, spotless maid,
Heav'n's sweetest joy, our hope, our aid.

II.

Fair lily, 'mid earth's sinful thorns,
Sweet dove, whose wings pure gold adorns,
Chaste Virgin, Root from whence there came
The Healer of our wounded frame.

III.

To thee we look, refulgent star,
To light us 'mid the world's dark war;

Strong tow'r against the dragon's wiles,
Protect us from his crafty smiles.

IV.

When toss'd upon life's stormy wave,
Oh! haste our wav'ring steps to save;
Oh! safely guide our wand'ring heart,
And drive away each hostile dart.

V.

Jesu, to Thee, the Virgin's Son,
Be never-ending homage done;
While to the Father we repeat
The same, .and to the Paraclete.

SAINT JOSEPH.

Te, Joseph, celebrent agminn cœlitum.

I.

Let angels chant thy praise, pure spouse of a pure bride,
  While earth's loud sounding choirs the joyous strains
    repeat,
To swell thy wondrous fame, to raise the pealing hymn,
    With which we all thy glory greet.

II.

When dark and bitter fears thy heavy heart oppress'd,
    And filled thy holy soul with sorrow and dismay,
An Angel quickly came, the wondrous secret told,
        And bringing peace, drove fear away.

III.

Thy arms thy new-born Lord with tender joy embrace,
    Him then to Egypt's land thy watchful care doth
       bring,
Him in Jerusalem lost, thou dost with love regain,
        And 'mid thy tears dost greet thy King.

IV.

When death's last pang is o'er do others gain their
    crown,
    But, Joseph, thine it was, and thine the lot alone,
While life did yet endure thy God to see and know,
        Like to the saints before his throne.

V.

Grant us, O Blessed Three, for Joseph's holy name,
    In highest bliss and love, above the stars to reign,
That we in joy with him may praise our loving God,
        And sing our glad eternal strain.

SAINT JOHN THE BAPTIST.

Ut queant laxis resonare fibris.

I.

That with glad voices, we thy matchless virtues,
  May, O great Baptist, through the world proclaim,
From sin's corruption free our lips declaring
      Thy glorious fame.

II.

From highest heaven an Angel bright descendeth,
  And to thy father doth make thy glory known ;
While all thy greatness, fame, and shining virtues,
      To him are shown.

III.

He weakly doubting, for his faith's purgation
  In mute amazement these wonders must behold,
Till speech returning, he thy advent hailing,
      God's high praises told.

IV.

Cloister'd in darkness, in the womb yet dwelling,
  Thee, the Lord's presence, with rapture did inspire ;
While those high parents sing their song of triumph,
      Filled with love's fire.

v.

Praise, fame, and blessing, to the Great Eternal,
With Thee, O Jesu, His co-eternal Son ;
Praise to the Spirit, through all ages living ;—
God, Three in One.

HOLY GUARDIAN ANGELS.

Custodes hominum psallimus Angelos.

I.

Oh! sing we now the praise of those blest spirits sent
To be our keepers here,—whom God our Father's love,
To guard our trembling steps, and ward away our
foes
Hath sent us down from Heav'n above.

II.

His own bright glory lost—with fierce and deadly hate
Th' apostate angel strives to drag us down from bliss,
To drag us from the thrones, for us by God rais'd up,
And drown our souls in hell's abyss.

III.

Then, watchful Spirit, haste, and quickly hither fly!
    Our country's woes avert, and be her keeper blest
Drive every ill away, each trouble calm and soothe,
           And give her peace and gentle rest.

IV.

Blest Trinity, to Thee, glad praise be ever sung,
    Who rul'st with power divine this mighty triple
        frame;
Oh! may thy glory spread, and endless days repeat
           The blessings sweet of thy dread name.

SAINT GABRIEL.

Christe, sanctorum decus Angelorum.

I.

O Christ, the glory of thy train angelic,
    Man's great Creator, his soul's Redeemer blest!
May we in triumph mount the seats eternal,
           And in glory rest.

II.

May valiant Michael peace around him shedding,
  From highest heaven come of its joys to tell,
In brightest vict'ry, by his arm confounding
        The powers of hell.

III.

May Gabriel coming, clad in shining armour,
  Crush the usurper, with standard high unfurl'd ;
And in glad triumph his glorious temples visit
        Through all the world.

IV.

May Raphael coming, he our woes' sweet healer,
  Soothe our afflictions with his heavenly skill;
All sickness curing, and our steps directing
        In virtue still.

V.

May the high Virgin, Queen of light and mercy,
  Quick come to aid us, and hear our bitter moan,
While the bright angels with glad anthems lead us
        To God's blessed throne.

VI.

Grant us this mercy, God of might and glory,
 Reigning for ever, Great Three in One above ;
While prostrate nations sing with joyous accents
 Hymns of praise and love.

SAINT RAPHAEL.

Tibi, Christe, Splendor Patris.

I.

Hail to Thee, the Father's brightness !
 Jesu, life and strength of all !
Mingling with thy joyous Angels,
 On thy saving name we call ;
While our hymns in flowing measure,
 In alternate cadence fall.

II.

Hail ! ye bright and blessed Spirits,
 Homage glad to you we pay ;
Hail ! O Raphael, friend, physician,
 Drive our evils far away :—
Thou the demon's potent victor,
 Ever be our guard and stay.

III.

May sweet Jesus list'ning to thee,
  Raise his dread and mighty arm;
Keep us ever pure and holy,
  Shield us safe from every harm;
Lead us to his own bright kingdom,
  Far from every dark alarm.

IV.

To the Great Almighty Father,
  Glory sing in anthems sweet;
Glory to our sweet Redeemer,
  Glory to the Paraclete;
To the God, for ever living,
  Three in One, glad praise repeat.

COMMON OF APOSTLES.

Exultet orbis gaudiis.

I.

Now let the Earth with joy be crown'd,
Let Heav'n the glorious strains resound;
Let Heav'n and Earth with joyous swell,
The great Apostles' praises tell.

II.

To you, the world's resplendent light,
Our Judges dread, 'mid glory bright,
Our fervent prayers in sorrow's hour,
With suppliant hearts, we humbly pour.

III.

At your behest, those portals high
Are quickly shut, or open fly;
We humbly pray you, now, that we
From sin's foul slav'ry may be free.

IV.

The power of life is in your hand,
And comes or goes at your command;
Oh! from our souls all stains efface,
Whilst healing virtues take their place.

V.

That when at that last solemn day,
Our Judge shall come in dread array.
We may with joy to you ascend,
To live in joys that never end.

VI.

To God the Father, and the Son,
And Holy Spirit, Three in One,
Be honour, glory, fame, and praise,
For never-ending length of days.

COMMON OF MANY MARTYRS.

Sanctorum meritis inclyta gaudia.

I.

Come loudly let us sing the deeds of martyr'd Saints,
 And tell the warfare dread, the conflict and the
  pain ;
Your mighty deeds, great Saints, with joyous hearts
 we sing,
  And in your praise intone our strain.

II.

These did the foolish world in its mad blindness spurn,
 Because they left it all, for Thee, their Lord and
  King ;
For Thee, with joy despis'd that fading, fleeting world
  That world so void, that fruitless thing.

For Thee, beneath their feet the pain they bravely trod,
    And for thy gentle love mid torments still were true;
The cruel iron hooks might piecemeal tear their flesh,
    But not their loving hearts subdue.

IV.

Beneath the slayer's sword like gentle lambs they fall,
    Without a murmur die, no sign of sorrow send,
But strong in brightest hope, in love enduring all,
    Their patience crowns their happy end.

V.

What tongue, O Jesu sweet, shall tell their love and joy,
    Shall tell the purest bliss for these thy Saints in store;
The Martyr's blessed palm upon each brow shall shine,
    And blossom there for evermore.

VI.

O Godhead, great and high, thy mercy sweet we claim,
    The Lord of all things made, our hearts' anointed
        King;
Give to thy servants peace, that we thy glorious fame,
    Through endless years in bliss may sing.

o

CONFESSORS.

Iste Confessor Domini, colentes.

I.

This Christ's Confèssor, whose high virtues telling
Through all the universe joyous tongues proclaim,
This day in triumph to his seat ascended
　　　　Glorious to reign.

II.

Pious and prudent, crown'd with gentle meekness,
Chaste, pure, and modest, was his life unstain'd
Mid works of mercy, by his deep devotion
　　　　Heaven he gain'd.

III.

Whenc'er he bent him o'er the bed of anguish,
O'er pains and sorrow, was his power made known;
All mis'ry ceasing, health and strength returning,
　　　　His glad presence own.

IV.

Hence in loud anthems, now his praises telling,
We pious trophies to him gladly raise,
Praying him humbly, still to guide and guard us,
　　　　Through all our days.

v.

Praise, might, and honour, to the Great Eternal,
Reigning in glory on his heavenly throne,
Ruling the universe by his mighty power,
    God Three in One.

VIRGINS.

Jesu, Corona Virginum.

I.

Jesu, the Virgins' crowning praise,
Receive the vows we humbly raise
To Thee, that chosen woman's Son,
Virgin and Mother both in one.

II.

Pure lilies pave thy path divine,
And spotless Virgins round Thee shine;
With joyous hymns they ever bless
The Stainless Spouse they now possess.

III.

Where'er thy steps mid glory tend,
Chaste Virgins on thy path attend,
With eager voice they gladly sing,
Their song of praise to thee their King.

IV.

On bended knees we crave thy love,
To draw our minds to things above,
To guard our senses and our heart
Safe from corruption's deadly dart.

V.

To God the Father, and the Son,
And Holy Spirit, Three in One,
Let honour glory, fame and praise,
Be sung for never-ending days.

HYMN FOR LENT.

Audi, benigne Conditor.

I.

O Gracious Maker, bend thine ears
Unto our prayers and bitter tears;
May we this fast in truth now keep,
Whilst thus we pray, and humbly weep.

II.

Thy piercing eye our hearts doth scan,
And measure all the woes of man ;
Whilst now, we sorrowing turn to Thee,
From sin's foul burthen set us free.

III.

Much have we sinn'd, and to excess,
But spare us, Lord, who thus confess ;
And for the glory of thy name,
Thy saving mercy now proclaim.

IV.

Whilst saving fasts our flesh subdue,
May thy sweet grace our hearts renew,
That vice may thus unfed remain,
And we from sin and guilt abstain.

V.

Grant us, O Sacred Trinity,
Grant us, O perfect Unity,
That these our fasts may fruitful prove
In endless bliss, in realms above.

EVENING HYMN.

Jam sol recedit igneus.

I.

Whilst fades the glowing sun away.
To Thee, sole source of light, we pray;
Blest Three in One, to every heart
The beams of life and love impart.

II.

At early dawn, at close of day,
To Thee, our homage glad we pay;
May we 'mid joys that never end,
With thy bright saints this homage tend

III.

To God the Father, and the Son,
And Holy Spirit, Three in One,
Be endless glory, as before
The world began, so evermore.

THE END.